HOLIDAY OF HOPE

PORT PROVIDENT: HURRICANE HOPE BOOK
THREE

KRISTEN ETHRIDGE

LAUREL LOCK PUBLISHING

A GIFT FOR YOU

Dear Reader,

You've heard of Army brats? Maybe you are one. Generally, their childhoods have one thing in common: living in a lot of different places.

I like to joke that I'm a retail brat. By the time I was eight years old, I'd lived in eight houses in six cities and attended four different schools.

My dad worked in retail, and as he got promoted up the chain, we moved. A lot.

And one thing about growing up in retail is that the holidays are always hectic. Thanksgiving? That's the day before Black Friday. Last minute Christmas shopping? Dad can't take you—he's making sure everyone else gets theirs done. A leisurely day after Christmas? Nope, December 26 is returns day!

You're always hoping for a good holiday season to carry you into the start of the year. And you're always at the mercy of the schedule. There are almost no Monday through Friday 9-5 roles in retail.

And I drew on that background as I got to know Jessica Bretton in Holiday of Hope. This is her world. Her memories are wrapped up in the store—and especially in Christmas. In the past, Christmas and the tourists of Port Provident had never let her down.

But now, after Hurricane Hope, things have changed. She's tried to keep all the plates spinning, but now they're crashing down on her and she feels powerless to do anything about it.

That is, until Bradley Thorpe gives her an idea.

Sometimes, all we need is one person to believe in us. Just one person can inspire and motivate us to get across the goal line.

The Bible says in Ecclesiastes that "if one falls down, his friend can help him up."

We all need a good friend who can help us see the power and beauty in ourselves.

I can't wait for you to meet Jessica and Bradley. I think we've all been in Jessica's shoes at one time or another. Who was there to lift you up?

This story may feel familiar because Port Provident isn't just a place, it's a place that's better because of you and how you connect with these stories. It's a community that you can be a part of every time you pick up one of these books. I think readers want more stories that are uplifting and make us think of the good in the world—because regardless of what the news tells us, it's out there. And that's why I created Port Provident—a town for all of us to visit for a sweet escape.

I'd like to invite you to join that reader community today. Just go to https://www.subscribepage.com/kristenethridgenewsletter. It's that easy!

One of my signature Sweet Escape Romances is Layla and Ridge's story, *A Place to Find Love*. Layla's spent her whole life searching for a greater meaning in her life. She comes to Port Provident running on fumes, but once she meets Ridge, she begins a journey that fills her with more than she ever hoped for—faith, family, and a place to find the love she's always longed for. I'll send you a copy just for joining my reader community, plus you'll be able to keep up with the latest on my books and Port Provident through regular emails and more reader bonuses.

Welcome to a Texas beachside town you can escape to anytime. I promise these stories will lift you up and leave you with a smile.

All the best,
Kristen

P.S… One of the best ways to get to know Port Provident even better is to get your *Passport to Port Provident*. It's a behind-the-scenes reader exclusive that's available when you join me on Facebook Messenger at www.facebook.com/kristenethridgebooks

www.kristenethridge.com
www.facebook.com/kristenethridgebooks
www.instagram.com/kristenethridge

1

———————

essica Bretton couldn't get away from it. Everywhere she could see, it was beginning to look a lot like Christmas. Every advertisement that popped up extolled the virtues of some must-have for the holiday season. Every weather forecast showed the temperature dipping lower across the country. Sometimes those reports were paired with photos of snow from other places like Colorado and New York. Thanksgiving had just passed yesterday, and the rest of America had plunged full-tilt into the most wonderful time of the year.

Indeed, it was beginning to look a lot like Christmas…everywhere but Bretton's on the Boardwalk in Port Provident, Texas.

Jessica was the fourth generation of her family to stand behind the cash register at Bretton's. She'd grown up in retail. She knew that today, the so-called "Black Friday," had received the moniker because it was the day retailers looked forward to changing their profit-and-loss sheets from red to black. From sweating paying the bills to cash flow. From the lean times to celebration.

This year, though, black more adequately described Jessica's mood.

Hurricane Hope crushed the island a few months ago and sent most

I

of the island into a mental and physical funk. The economic toll of the storm couldn't fully be calculated yet.

Jessica had once loved fall and the lead-up to the store's most profitable season of the year—the holiday season. This year, fall had disappeared into a blur of mucking out and contractors and rebuilding—to say nothing of feverish negotiations and disputes with insurance companies and a mad rush to restock Bretton's decimated inventory before the holiday shoppers came calling.

Except, despite all of Jessica's long nights and high levels of stress to get everything back and running, the holiday shoppers weren't coming.

They weren't calling.

They weren't caroling.

The only thing they were doing was staying away. The new mayor, Angela Ruiz, had made the rounds of the major Texas television stations last week, announcing that Port Provident was back open for business.

As far as Jessica could tell, though, Mayor Ruiz's words had all fallen on deaf ears. The bell on the door of Bretton's on the Boardwalk was not ringing. It was not jangling. And it was definitely not jingling. In a shop dedicated to Christmas all year long, this year, there was very little Christmas spirit to be found anywhere.

Just then, the small tinny clang of the bell over the door did break into Jessica's loop of depressed thoughts. She looked up from the bleak spreadsheet she'd been studying. "Welcome to Bretton's. How may I help you?"

"Hey, Jess—it's just me."

Bradley Thorpe, the director of the Port Provident Park Board, stood just inside the doorway.

Jessica wouldn't lie, it was always nice to see Bradley—in a "steal a quick glance of the hot guy" kind of way—but she knew he wasn't here to buy an ornament of a sand dollar dressed as Santa. He might be a momentary distraction, but he wasn't going to fix the problem that was clearly laid out in black-and-white on the spreadsheet in front of her.

Still, she couldn't skip Bretton's expectations of customer service just because Bradley wasn't actually a customer. "Hey Bradley—what can I help you with today?"

"Nothing, really—I just need to take this poster down." He pointed at the broadsheet-sized advertisement in the window.

"But that's the Santas on the Street poster." Jessica didn't understand. "Santas on the Street" was a staple of the holiday season in Port Provident. People came to the island one night a year, dressed up as St. Nick. They rode bikes around to local restaurants and stores, leaving money in cash registers and canned food in donation bins. It usually turned into a bit of a wild time for the party-going Santas, but overall it was positive for the island and the merchants who called Port Provident home. "Why are you taking it down? Your crew just put it up last week."

"They've canceled it," Bradley said matter-of-factly.

Jessica felt her heart turn to an icicle in her chest. "Cancelled it? Who? Why?"

"City Manager's office. Colin said that after further review, we just don't have the resources or the manpower to put this on. We don't have enough police on the streets to keep our citizens safe right now. We can't police thousands of tourists—if they show up—and we can't afford the overtime, anyway."

Bradley began to pick at the strips of tape holding the poster against the window.

"So, are we doing anything for Christmas, Bradley?" The icicle in her heart began to stretch and reach through her veins. She practically began to shiver.

"Well, I'm sure families will still celebrate. But as a city, I don't think so, no."

Jessica's tongue flapped like a penguin's flipper. She could barely talk. "But what about Mayor Ruiz's public goodwill tour? Aren't we supposed to be open for business?"

"We're open for business, Jessica. That hasn't changed."

She shook her head. "No, we're not. If we're not going to extend the same hospitality Port Provident has always extended at one of our biggest times of the year, then we're not really open for business. We're a tourist town, Bradley. We're not open for business unless we're making it easy for tourists to come do business with us."

He wadded up the poster into a ball. It crunched between his hands, and the sound of crackling paper rang in Jessica's ears like an emergency siren.

Fitting. She may as well just call a code blue. Four generations of Bretton family members had stewarded this store through a century, and two years after getting handed over to Jessica, the store went into cardiac arrest.

RIP Bretton's on the Boardwalk. It was nice knowing you.

"We'll be back next year, Jessica. These things just take time." He casually tossed the ball of paper from his right hand to his left. "Do you have a trashcan?"

There was a small, rectangular trashcan behind the counter. It held unwanted receipts, mismarked price tags, and the occasional empty to-go cup of iced tea quite nicely.

But she was going to need a larger one now to hold the trashing of her family's dream.

Jessica leaned down and picked up the small gray bin. "You can use this."

Bradley reached his arm back and shot the paper ball in an arc toward the trashcan. It hit the mark squarely, making a soft swish as the paper scraped the side of the plastic bag that lined the inside of the can.

Today was the blackest Friday ever.

Bradley dug through his pocket for some change to leave behind as a tip at Café Provident. He'd just pulled down the Santas on the Street poster from their front window, and he needed a cup of coffee to warm up the chill that had lingered in his veins since his stop at Bretton's on the Boardwalk.

Canceling the slightly-chaotic Santa Parade was in the best interest of the Island right now. He knew that. The night always progressed from a fun opportunity to drop off toys and food to be donated to local charities and wound up as a pilgrimage through the bars and other nightlife of Port Provident. Someone always decided to be Superman. And this year, Port Provident just couldn't afford the chance that something could get out of hand.

But he'd seen the look in Jessica's crisp blue eyes. A mix of shock and desperation, Bradley had been unable to shake the memory of her obvious distress as he'd continued down the block, pulling posters from shop windows and bulletin boards.

"You gonna order?" The barista behind the counter looked squarely at Bradley. The shortness in the young woman's voice made Bradley feel as though he were back in grade school, being summoned to the front of the class to write his name on the board in crisp, white chalk.

He dropped his extra dollar and spare change in the tip jar, hoping that seeing a gratuity up front would placate the coffee crafter. "I just need a large coffee, black."

The barista scribbled notes with a permanent marker on the side of the thick paper cup. "Lilly will take care of you at the end of the counter."

He handed a five-dollar bill to the young woman. "Keep the change," he said as he walked to the end to wait for his coffee.

The sullen attitude of both of the workers depressed him. It was the same feeling he got when he'd been in Bretton's on the Boardwalk earlier. Was there really no Christmas cheer in Port Provident this year?

The thought weighed on him more heavily than he wanted it to. As the head of the Park Board of Port Provident, Bradley's role was primarily oversight of the beaches and public parks, but overall, it was grounded in promoting the tourism of Provident Island and ensuring those tourists were safe and had a pleasant experience while in town.

There was no denying that Hurricane Hope's landfall had changed the game for the residents, tourists, and business owners of Port Provident. And Bradley fully understood why the City Council pulled the plug on this year's Santa event—with everything else the city had absorbed since mid-September, Port Provident could not afford to absorb the consequences of Santas who might get out of control for one night. Control was tenuously maintained right now—many island residents were still in temporary housing and while, overall, the city was moving in the right direction toward recovery—nothing fit the definition of "normal."

The barista called out Bradley's name, breaking his lumbering train of thought.

"Oh, I need to grab that too," he said, as he reached for the steaming cup of coffee.

"Grab what?" The barista gave him a hooded glance.

"Your other Santas on the Street poster—the one behind you. I got the one in the window as I came in. It's been canceled this year, so I'm taking all the posters down."

Now the cashier joined the conversation. "Cancelled? You can't cancel Santas on the Street. It's tradition."

The pit of Bradley's stomach felt as deep as the Grand Canyon. He parroted out the same response he'd already given a dozen times today. "Well, it wasn't my decision. The City Council decided we just don't have the infrastructure to support it this year."

The cashier mumbled something to the barista. And while Bradley didn't understand everything she'd just said, he had picked out a few choice words that more than adequately summed up what she thought of City Council and their plan.

"Really, I am sorry. Everything will be back to normal next year— at least it should be."

The cashier pushed a lock of hair under a slouchy knitted beanie. "Yeah, I don't think you guys at City Hall understand how much we count on events like Santas on the Street to give people a reason to come and shop here. How am I supposed to buy Christmas gifts for my kid this year? I'm a single mom."

Her words were hotter than the cup of coffee in Bradley's hand.

"Well, shopping local is a great thing, but I think it would be fine if you went to the mall on the mainland this year."

She shot Bradley a look that told him clearly where he could go and how he could get there. Bradley glanced down at his shoes, certain he'd just stepped in a big pile of reindeer poop.

"I didn't say *where*. I said *how*. That's our biggest night in December here. The tips I make from Santas on the Street pay for my Christmas presents. Scroogey City Council just ruined my Christmas." She turned and ripped the poster off the bulletin board behind the register and threw it on the counter then stomped off, wiping her left eye from behind the thick black frames of her glasses.

Great. He'd made her cry.

Well, not him, specifically. City Council had. But as he'd been reminded a few times during his career, he served at the pleasure of City Council. So, it was really all the same thing.

Bradley lifted the coffee cup with one hand and dragged the ripped poster toward him with two fingers from his other hand. He pinched it and wadded it into a tight ball. With some ribbon on top, it could have been an ornament on a tree.

But not this year. Not in this town.

Bradley Scrooge had come to town, not Santa Claus.

Jessica stubbed her toe on a segment of sidewalk that had shifted upwards. Yet another roadblock the hurricane had thrown in her way, she thought to herself as she walked and tried to ignore the sting.

She hurried up the steps to the Provident Memorial Library, weighed down with a heavy shopping bag in each hand. The sun was setting in the sky, and Jessica knew the staff would soon be locking the doors to the building—she hoped she could squeak her delivery in before the key turned.

"Jessica! You brought them!" Anita Sullivan opened the massive front door to the large Victorian building. Four stories tall and with a sturdy stone façade, the library's look and feel took all who saw it back to a different era. The Provident Memorial Library had been an important architectural and community fixture in Port Provident for more than a century.

Anita had been a fixture at the library for almost half a century, and Jessica's heart thawed a little as she saw the excitement on the face of the woman who had brought so much joy to children, readers, and amateur historians alike on the island.

"They were way up in storage at Bretton's. I hope this is what you were looking for."

"Oh, I'm sure it will be perfect, Jessica. I was so excited when Donna said she thought she'd seen them in the attic while doing some post-hurricane clean up." The gray-haired lady waved broadly with her left arm. "Come in, come in! Let's lock up the doors and take a look."

Jessica followed Anita through the library—around bookcases, down hallways, through reading rooms, and behind large tables perfect for holding an afternoon's discoveries or research. At last, they came to Anita's spacious office on the third floor.

"Ok, put the bags right there." Anita rubbed her hands together with delight. "I can't wait any longer to see all these."

No sooner had Jessica placed the bags on the table, Anita dove in, pulling out several white boxes. Gently, she lifted the lid on each—then she paused. "I need my gloves."

She walked to her desk and opened a drawer, pulling out two pairs of clean white gloves. "One for you, one for me."

Anita handed a pair to Jessica, then slid her small hands into a pair that had clearly seen regular use.

She delicately picked up a photo mounted on thick paper and sighed. "Oh, just lovely. Look at that detail."

Jessica leaned in. "So… what is all of this?"

"This," Anita said with a smile that glowed like no sterile overhead light could ever hope to, "this is our history. This is how Port Provident celebrated Christmas when she was the jewel of the Gulf Coast."

Jessica gingerly touched the photo. A woman sat in a sleigh with two children. A fur wrapped her shoulders, and her hands were bundled in a large muff. Each of the children wore thick coats and a scarf around the neck. A man in a formal suit stood behind them.

In spite of the obvious Victorian charm, something didn't seem quite right.

"Wait a minute. That's the Thacker house."

Anita nodded. "The 1897 Thacker House—and that's the Thacker family, all bundled up for a cold winter's night…except that the palm tree behind them appears to be in grand form. Mrs. Thacker is probably sweating under all her furs and wraps and hats."

"That's funny, but very true. I think I wore flip-flops to Christmas dinner last year," Jessica said, still studying the serious faces from generations ago. "I guess Mrs. Thacker would never have done that."

"Not at all. Her husband established First Provident Bank. She had one of the most coveted social positions in town. In fact, she chaired the Port Provident Ladies' Musicale Society, the founders of the annual Christmas Carol Celebration that ran in Port Provident for many years, from 1890. The Great Storm of 1910 blew it away—just like almost everything else in town. The joy was gone from this city for years as they rebuilt."

"Kind of like today," Jessica said, almost hiding the words under her breath.

"What did you say?" Anita reached in the box and pulled out photos of a stage production. A tall man was wrapped in strips of cloth and draped in chains. She tapped the man with the tip of her finger. "Jacob Marley was always played by Walter Mitchell. He was the tallest man in town—almost six-foot-seven, which was almost unheard of for the time."

Jessica leaned over to see the detail more closely. He very much looked like the specter of Dickens' tale. "I said it feels like 1910 all over again. There's no Christmas cheer on Port Provident this year, either."

Anita laid the photo down. "How so? I've seen far more decorations out than I thought I'd see, considering it's only the day after Thanksgiving."

Jessica let out a cold, tight breath that had been hiding behind her sternum. She told Anita about the almost non-existent sales at Bretton's on the Boardwalk and her fears for the store.

"And then Bradley Thorpe from the Park Board came by today and took down the Santas on the Street posters—the city has canceled the one Christmas activity I was counting on in order to pay my bills this month. I don't know what I'm going to do, Anita. The insurance money isn't going to be enough to cover our losses—and that process is like a trickle of slow progress, when there is any progress. There are no tourists. There are no shoppers. And there is no ring to my cash register. I've talked with some of the other downtown merchants. I'm not the only one. I understand that Santas on the Street can get kind of crazy—that part always annoyed me—but we needed it. The people like me who depend on Christmas sales need something, anything to get people back to the island in December."

"Sounds like you need a little Tiny Tim in your life."

"'God bless us, every one.' Tim's sentiment sounds perfectly lovely, but I don't see it happening this year. But if it doesn't happen this year, Bretton's is done. And it will happen on my watch." Jessica's head slouched downward with the weight of failing generations of her family.

She didn't want to think about it, but she had to prepare for the worst.

Closing the doors to Bretton's on the Boardwalk forever.

"Before you go, Jessica, I've got something I want you to take with you." Anita sweetly patted Jessica's gloved hand with her own. "Wait right here."

The older woman left her gloves stacked next to the photos and padded out the door.

As she waited, Jessica gingerly picked up more photos and looked through them. All visions from Port Provident's heyday, they showed scenes from a performance of A Christmas Carol, people dressed in their Sunday best and gathered around a banquet table, and even Port Provident residents on the streets of downtown enjoying a snack of real chestnuts that had been roasted over a fire. If she wasn't mistaken, they were standing in front of the steps to the building that now housed Bretton's on the Boardwalk.

The scenes immortalized in tones of sepia seemed so charming, so quaint, so perfect.

It tugged at her heart to realize that things were not that perfect anymore. She remembered playing in the store as a child with her grandparents, then later helping out as a teenager when her parents ran the store. So many memories. But in all reality, there wouldn't be many more.

The click of the doorknob announced Anita's return before she stepped in the room. Jessica took the nanosecond to push down her emotions.

"Here you go, Jessica." Anita held out a book. The cover was cloth, shiny with wear and slightly frayed on the corners. "It's a book all about the Victorian holiday celebrations here in Port Provident. It was published by the Ladies' Musicale Society—and I am inclined to think that Mrs. Thacker was one of the primary authors of the book. Maybe there's some Christmas cheer in here that will still ring true, even today."

Jessica held the book carefully. She could smell a very faint mustiness, like so many older books tended to give off. Gingerly, she opened the book and flipped through a few pages. There was even a section of elaborate sketches in the middle of the book.

"Thank you, Anita. I'll bring it back soon."

She didn't really plan to spend much time with the book, charming as it appeared to be. She just wanted to go home and go to sleep—and spend as much time with the covers over her head until the inevitable happened and she locked Bretton's doors for good. In spite of that, she appreciated Anita's attempts to raise her spirits.

"Keep it as long as you need to, my dear. I know you'll take good care of it."

Jessica tucked the book into a pocket in her purse and forced down the lump in her throat that formed as she realized her family had once said they knew she'd take good care of Bretton's on the Boardwalk, too.

At least she trusted herself not to let Anita down. She didn't have that level of confidence about any other promises she'd made.

Bradley arrived at the Park Board office early to go over some insurance paperwork that had come in yesterday.

He'd skipped his usual stop for a cup of black coffee, though, and the morning was dragging. He couldn't face the stern disapproval from behind the counter at Café Provident again.

The loud knock at his door jolted him like a shot of super-concentrated caffeine. The office had been completely quiet. He took a deep breath before calling for the unknown knocker to open the door and come in.

If the knock had surprised him, the visitor about dropped him out of his chair.

He'd come to the office this morning expecting a morning reviewing highly technical insurance language regarding repairs on several buildings on the beach owned by the Park Board. He had certainly not expected the very determined face of Jessica Bretton to appear in his doorway.

"I have a proposal for you." She wasted no time crossing the gray carpet and getting in front of his desk. Jessica placed a small green book on top of the pile of paperwork in the middle of Bradley's desk.

The tone of her voice told Bradley he had no choice but to listen.

"Okay?" Bradley wasn't sure what else to say. He decided that just letting her do the talking was the best plan.

"We need to bring Christmas back to the island, Bradley. It's not just going to come by itself. I read this whole book last night. I couldn't put it down. I know what we need to do."

He raised his hands, flipping them over in an empty gesture. "It wasn't my call, Jessica. I know this is hard on you and everyone downtown, but there's nothing I can do about it."

She sat in the chair closest to the desk and leaned forward with intent. "I've thought about it and I agree to cancel the Santa night was the right move. By the time I close my store, it's become a bar hop, and then the police have to babysit grownups for the rest of the night. I understand we can't afford the risk of an event like that. But what if we did something that focused on families? Something that involved our own Port Provident families?"

She tapped the book with one manicured nail. Bradley couldn't help but notice the red polish with white diagonal stripes like little candy cane bites at the end of each finger.

"But why the book?" Bradley couldn't help but ask the primary question on his mind.

"Before the 1910 hurricane, Port Provident hosted a celebration of Dickens' *A Christmas Carol.* It was a contemporary celebration at the time—*A Christmas Carol* was a very popular book that had come out in the mid-1800s. In 1890, the ladies of the town put on a community play of *A Christmas Carol.* Over the years to come, it evolved with a street parade, chestnuts roasting over open fires, and even visits from British royalty. People from across the community made it happen, and then people started coming from far and wide to take part."

Bradley shook his head. "That sounds cool, but I don't understand what you want to do."

"I want to bring it back." She locked her blue eyes on his face. He felt the pierce of her stare like the point of an icicle.

"But how, Jessica? You don't just throw together an event like that on the fly. We plan all year for our major events in the city. And while you're right, the crowd would likely be more tame, I just don't think the city can handle any big crowds of any kind right now."

She picked up the book and held it gently with her candy cane fingertips. Jessica opened it to a section of lavish illustrations. "Look at these. This was Port Provident's heyday. What if we could bring that back? What if we could bring some hope and holiday cheer to the people in our city?"

Bradley could understand why she was so taken with the idea. The illustrations looked like they were straight out of those Christmas cards his mother used to find so charming—Carrier and Chive?

He shook his head. *No, that wasn't right. What were they called?* He began to vaguely hum a tune.

"So, you're not even willing to give it a try?"

"Wait, what?" Bradley didn't understand the knife-edge of frustration in her voice.

"You shook your head."

"Oh, I was just trying to remember something that these

illustrations reminded me of. Old Christmas cards my mother used to love."

She traced the face of a woman immortalized on the stage. "Like Currier and Ives, right?"

Bradley let out a chuckle. "That's the name. I couldn't think of it. Carrier and Chive stuck in my head. I knew that was more like the name for a loaded baked potato, not iconic art."

"And it's a little early to be thinking about lunch." She smiled. "But if you'll help me with this, the potato is on me."

"I work for the government. I can't take bribes."

"Can a carb really be a bribe, Bradley?"

Bradley tried not to laugh at her, but her tone was completely serious. "I'd need to consult the manual."

"So, you're saying there's hope?" The look in her eyes had softened, and he could see a little golden flicker on the edge of the iris.

He didn't want to disappoint her—especially since he knew he'd tanked her day yesterday—but there wasn't much encouragement to give.

"I wish I could, Jessica, but it really isn't my call. There's a City Council meeting tomorrow. You could try and get on the agenda and see what they think. That's my best advice right there."

She picked up the book and tucked it back in her purse, then gave her lower lip two distinct chews. A twinkle in her eye brought back more Christmas memories of long ago, this time of stories of Santa Claus and the joy and mischief he carried with him.

"So… you're saying there's hope."

2

Jessica looked through the windows of Bretton's as she passed by. She saw Donna behind the cash register, but other than that, not a creature was stirring inside the shop. Jessica would have been grateful for a mouse today—especially if the mouse had brought an AmEx card.

Normally, Jessica would have popped in the store. She would have stocked some merchandise, straightened some shelves, then gone back to her office in the corner of the stockroom for an hour or two to catch up on the never-ending pile of paperwork.

But not today.

Today she was on a mission, one every bit as determined and frantic as Santa's one-night-only trip around the world to bring holiday cheer.

She would put together a plan to bring back the joy of Christmas past to Port Provident. She would get in front of the City Council tomorrow. And she would not fail to convince them that her idea was just what Port Provident needed.

She just wasn't quite sure how.

Armed with the book on loan from Anita and a folder full of other notes and copies of photographs Anita had pulled together for her this morning, Jessica ducked into Café Provident for something warm. Surveying the menu, written with swirls and stripes and other whimsy on a chalkboard, Jessica decided on a hot chocolate as she stepped to the counter.

"Marshmallows or whipped cream?"

Jessica knew most of the people behind the beverages at Café Provident, but this face was new.

"Mmm. Marshmallows, please." She smiled at the thought of the fluffy clouds melting into the warm cocoa. "I'm Jessica. Are you new here?"

The blonde nodded. "This is my first day. I'm Emily."

"It's nice to meet you. Are you new to Port Provident?" As a lifelong resident of the island, getting her degree at Provident College, and working at her family's store since childhood, Jessica always said she'd seen just about every face on the island at one time or another—but Emily's clear complexion and braids framing each side of her face were not ringing any bells.

"About a year. I came here to do PR for PYT—the Provident Youth Theatre company—but since the hurricane, my hours have been cut. We don't think we'll be able to do a show until the spring, at the earliest. I just needed something to make up the difference."

Jessica's brain began to spin as Emily introduced herself.

"PYT? Why are you not able to put on shows? Is the theatre badly damaged? I thought I'd read there was actually minimal damage."

"There was. We're very fortunate—everything is cleaned up and back to normal in the building, for the most part. But good luck getting anyone to come to Port Provident right now. There's been so much progress and rebuilding here since Hurricane Hope, but people in Houston and other places think we're still a disaster zone. We just don't see that we'd be able to get a return on our expenses for putting on a show until early next year."

Jessica nodded. She understood the bleak picture and the numbers game all too well.

"What about a one-time thing, more of a community event?"

Emily poured hot milk in the cup she'd designated for Jessica, then swirled chocolate in it. "What do you mean? I don't know of any community events going on. Everything has been so quiet here since Hurricane Hope."

"Exactly. But what if there was a way to change all that? Do you think PYT might be interested?"

A garnish of small marshmallows topped the hot chocolate. Once the lid was secured on the cup, Emily handed it to Jessica.

"I'd certainly talk to Denise about it. I know she's dying to get back to business in any way we can."

"I'm going to sit right over there by the window." Jessica pointed to a table in the corner with room to spread out her notes and research. "If you have a break or things slow down and you want to talk about what's on my mind, so you can go to Denise…come on over, and we'll chat."

About thirty minutes later, Emily slipped in the chair across from Jessica. "So tell me more about your idea."

Jessica pulled out the copies of photos that Anita had sent and started walking Emily through the history of the long-ago celebrations and community-driven play of *A Christmas Carol*. As Jessica noted different aspects of the event and how she thought they could modernize it, she noticed a light begin to flicker in Emily's eyes.

"I've got several of my reporter contacts who are just waiting for PYT to reopen so they can do a story on it. I could definitely call them up to cover this and help us promote it." Emily paused. "Beth, come over here and listen to this. Jessica, could Beth have some kind of booth for Café Provident out at the event?"

Jessica couldn't stop the smile that pushed across her face. "Wassail, cider, hot chocolate…chestnuts roasting on an open fire. If you can do any of that, Beth, you can have as many booths as you'd like."

Beth Greenling, the owner of Café Provident, stood just behind Emily. "We can do all of that, Jessica. And more. I wish we could do a special high tea. How British and fun would that be?"

Jessica raised her hands in an open gesture. "Why can't we? If you can dream it up and we can get the idea green-lighted, I say the sky is the limit."

"So how do we get the idea green-lighted?" Beth wiped her hands on the Christmas-themed apron that covered her street clothes.

Like a reindeer pulling up to another chimney, Jessica's enthusiasm came to a quick stop. "Well, that's the catch. We have to convince City Council that this won't be an event with the potential to be out-of-control like Santas on the Street. There's a meeting tomorrow. Can you come with me?"

"Absolutely. Can I bring a few others with me?"

"The more, the merrier," Jessica replied. "At least I ho-ho-hope so."

"The lady at the front desk told me I'd find you out here." Jessica held a brown paper bag in her outstretched arms. "This is for you."

The sound of Jessica's voice broke through the silence, startling him. Bradley stepped out from behind the new playground set that had just been installed at the small beachside park. He was touring several of the Park Board's properties this afternoon, checking renovation progress.

"What's in there?" He eyed the bag skeptically before reaching out a hand.

"A potato."

He couldn't help himself from laughing at the matter-of-fact tone in her voice. "A potato?"

"Yes. With Carrier and Chive. Or something like that. I told you lunch was on me if I could enlist your help."

Bradley unrolled the top of the bag and looked inside. Sure enough, there was a three-dimensional oval, wrapped in foil. Small disposable containers of cheddar cheese, bacon, and more than one container of chives had been tossed in on top, along with some napkins and a plastic fork.

"Jessica, as much as I'd love to eat this potato—I just don't think I can help you. The City Council has spoken. I work for them. I can't just thumb my nose at the people who sign my paycheck."

She let out a deep breath. "Don't go bacon my heart, Bradley."

He wanted to laugh, but inside he could feel a corner of his heart crumble. He'd tried a hundred different ways to ask Jessica Bretton out in the last year or so, but she'd always been so focused on her responsibilities at the store that she'd declined every single invitation. He'd finally given up—and had gone out of his way to avoid her, so he wasn't tempted to look foolish by asking her out again. Yesterday was the first time he'd walked into Bretton's for months.

Now, she needed something from him, and there was nothing he could do about it.

That simple fact gave him a bigger headache than all the insurance paperwork he'd seen since Hurricane Hope's September landfall. He'd spent plenty of time praying for a chance to get to be more to Jessica Bretton. This seemed more like a cruel joke than the answer he'd been hoping for.

"I *ham* trying not to, Jessica." He decided the best thing to do was to just play along. It would be far easier to talk about cured pork products than to ever let Jessica on to the crush he'd been harboring for longer than he cared to admit. "But it's a conflict of interest."

She frowned, and the filtered sunlight caught the furrow of her brow, highlighting the lines that ran across her forehead.

"There's nothing you can tell me? Not even a tip or a hint?" Jessica glanced briefly at her feet. "That just sounds desperate, doesn't it? I'm sorry, Bradley. I don't mean to put you in a bad spot. I'm just…I'm in a bad place. I can't eat, I can't sleep. I can't think about anything except the tiny number in the Bretton's bank account. I'm almost to the point where I can't pay the store's bills. And since the store pays me, if I can't pay those bills and make payroll, then I can't pay my own bills either."

Bradley put the sack with the potato on the table nearby. He had to battle his instincts. He wanted to give her a hug. He wanted to do something to reassure her that everything would be okay.

The problem was, he didn't know whether or not everything would be okay. He knew she had a lot of enthusiasm for this Victorian Christmas idea. Plus, he could see how a family-friendly event made far more sense than a long night of Santas on the Street. But he didn't know how he could be her advocate on this. It would be overstepping his bounds.

Things at City Hall had gotten tight since the hurricane. With so much scrutiny from so many organizations regarding red tape and rebuilding, the city government was going above and beyond to be seen as checking the boxes and playing by the rules.

And speaking of playing by the rules, Bradley steeled his arms to remain at his side.

Hugging Jessica—even as good-natured reassurance and nothing more—was not in the rules. She clearly wasn't interested in him, and he just had to accept that and abide by it.

He saw the droop of her shoulders and the slouch of her head. Everything about her posture screamed a silent cry of emotional pain. He had to at least find something to say to give her some hope.

"When you do pitch it to them, be sure and help them understand that it's a partnership between the merchants and show them clearly who is onboard. I don't know if they fully understand how make-or-break this seems to be for many of you."

Slowly, Jessica lifted her head. "Do you think that could change their minds?"

Again, he wanted to reassure her—to tell her everything would be okay. But he had to be honest, and the honest truth was he just didn't know. "Anything is really possible. But I don't think it's going to hurt you to show a united front with other business owners."

She wiped a finger below her left eye. Bradley hadn't even realized tears had escaped. "I can do that. It really isn't just me."

He thought back to that very uncomfortable stop for a cup of coffee. "I know it's not. I just wish there was more I could do. I wish things were more of how they used to be. Before the hurricane, I had the freedom to pull a few strings. But now, with the feds watching everything we do and tying even the most benign things into whether or not we get approved for certain recovery funds—I can't do my job the way I'm used to doing it."

Bradley couldn't put his finger on it, but even his own roles and responsibilities at the Park Board seemed to be in some kind of flux. He certainly wasn't going to bring up his own uncertainties, though. His concerns felt more abstract—he could tell something was different, but he didn't know what.

Jessica's were real. As in black and white on a spreadsheet real.

"I know. I'm sorry for putting you in a hard place, Bradley. I really don't mean to. I just…" She let her thought trail off like the roll of a wave reaching up onto the shore. "Anyway, I hope you enjoy the potato."

She tried to put a smile on her face.

"I'll probably rus*set* down at the table and eat it shortly. Get it? Russet, sit…"

Bradley noticed that Jessica had hesitated in getting the right words out for most of their conversation, but she didn't stall one second in rolling her eyes at Bradley's poor attempt at a joke.

"Awful, right?" he asked.

"Don't quit your day job. Standup comedy is not in your future."

After she'd walked off, Bradley sat down at the picnic table and pulled the potato and garnishes out of the bag. He could see Jessica's car turning out of the parking lot and on to Gulfview Boulevard. He followed the little red hatchback with his eyes until it was out of sight.

Standup comedy likely wasn't his future, but he wished something different was—he wished Jessica Bretton was.

"I'm glad you're here a little early, Bradley." Mayor Pro-Tem Carter Porter caught up to Bradley the next afternoon as soon as he came through the door of the City Council chambers ahead of the scheduled meeting. "Can you step over into the other room with me?"

Carter gestured at a double door just to the left of the dais where the Port Provident City Council sat during their public meetings. The doors led to a private room where they could have discussions which met the requirements to be held behind closed doors.

Bradley could feel sweat begin to dampen his palms. He couldn't place what Carter Porter would possibly want to talk to him about—and anything that did come to mind wasn't good.

He followed behind Carter and let the echo of his shoes on the tile floor do all the talking. He couldn't think of any words to start the conversation with. Small talk about the weather probably wasn't called for.

Carter closed the doors carefully behind them, then walked over to one of the tables in the center of the room and leaned against it. "We're announcing some changes at the meeting today."

Bradley nodded. His palms continued to generate sweat, like humidity after a summer rainstorm. "I figured you weren't inviting me back here to offer me a raise."

"Nobody's getting a raise this year—but you're a department head. You know that. The hurricane washed all those hopes away." Carter drummed his fingers over the edge of the table. "But I am offering you a new opportunity."

This felt worse than he could have imagined. Carter's voice was way too serious for this to be an option Bradley would be excited about. The hesitation he heard in Carter's words spoke volumes. It clearly said Carter was searching for the right words to put on a sell-job.

"New, huh? Not better, not good? New." May as well just come right out with it, Bradley thought.

"Well, we hope you'll think it's good."

Hope. Yeah, just like the last round of Hope that hit Port Provident —Hurricane Hope—this wasn't going to end well. Bradley brushed his palms down the front of his khakis.

"Try me." Bradley couldn't muster a third syllable of enthusiasm.

"You know restrictions are being tied to this recovery money, right?"

Bradley nodded. The red tape was long, it was sticky, and it was knotted tighter than something the Coast Guard would use to secure a ship.

"Well, we're having to—ahem—bring efficiencies to our departmental structure." Carter paused with a slight roll of his eyes. "We've had some outside consultants working on how best we can achieve the hurdles that the government has placed in front of us. We've settled on a set of recommendations we're prepared to accept, and one of those affects the Park Board."

Bradley braced himself for the punch and hoped it wouldn't be a total knockout.

"Go on," he said skeptically.

"We will be combining the Park Board with the Convention and Visitors Bureau—pulling our tourist-focused departments under one umbrella."

Bradley wasn't sure what he'd been expecting, but it wasn't this. "Okay, so will the CVB be moving into our offices? And I guess Deborah is now reporting to me?"

"Not exactly." Carter shrugged one shoulder. "The way things have to go—at least for now—is that the Park Board is being absorbed into the CVB. You're going to report to Deborah."

Bradley's palms were no longer sweaty. Now they were on fire. So was every inch of his skin. In fact, he briefly reached up and patted one hand on top of his hair.

No, there were no actual flames leaping out of his head.

It felt good to confirm that minor detail since all body temperature evidence seemed to point to the contrary.

"This isn't an *opportunity*, Carter. This is a demotion. A big slap in the face." He pointed a finger in Carter's direction. "And you know it, or you wouldn't have brought me in this closed-door area to tell me."

Carter held up both hands in the age-old gesture of deflection. "It should only be temporary. We just have to get through this rebuilding and get to the next phase."

Bradley clenched his jaw against the thoughts in his head. He could not say what he was thinking. Talk about a career-limiting move. Not that it would matter much. The Number Two person in city government had just been very clear about what the powers-that-be in Port Provident thought of his career.

"I'm not a party planner, Carter." Bradley bit out the words.

"No one is saying you are, Bradley. And you and I both know that's not what the CVB does, either."

Bradley couldn't keep his eyebrow from raising. *"Tomato, to-mah-to.* Look, I'm sure they do great work. But my team and I keep your greatest asset running. We keep the beaches clean, safe and well-managed. Who is booking conventions if the beach is a mess? I think you have the order of things backward, Carter. The CVB should be reporting into the Park Board."

Carter sidestepped, then moved away from the table. "I don't necessarily disagree with you, Bradley. But for now, we have to abide by the consultant group's recommendations. That's basically all there is to it. We're between a rock and a hard place. We have to have those recovery funds. We can't jeopardize them."

Collateral damage.

That's what Bradley realized his career had become.

He couldn't keep a bitter sigh of disgust from filling the space between him and Carter before turning around and walking out of the room. Bradley wished he could go anywhere but the City Council chambers.

He wanted to sit anywhere but his usual seat on the second row.

He wanted to look at anything but the other directors of the various city departments, knowing he was technically no longer one of them.

He thought about just standing at the back of the room, quietly biding his time until Mayor Angela Ruiz dropped the gavel to close the meeting.

Then he saw blonde hair, a green cable knit sweater and a pair of jeans with a wash so dark they appeared to be midnight.

Bradley actually couldn't just bide his time and then sneak out—he was required to be at these meetings. But all of a sudden, he realized he really didn't want to go anywhere. He wasn't the only one who had a lot riding on the decisions of the group of elected officials taking their seats on the dais.

Well, if no one stood up for him when the decisions about his career, at least there would be one person to stand up for Jessica Bretton when it came time for City Council to decide the fate of her business.

He didn't have anything to lose anymore—and he knew she had everything at stake.

There were several seats saved on the second row for those who had official agenda items. Jessica held a copy of the agenda tightly in her hand. Her name stood out clearly at the top of the speaker list. She walked toward the front of the room, giving a small, covert wave to Emily and Beth from Café Provident as she passed them. There were several other familiar faces in the crowd, owners of small businesses from across the historic district. And in the third row, she saw Anita.

Anita provided the inspiration for this whole wild and crazy idea. She knew Anita wasn't scheduled to speak and she wasn't a business owner who could weigh in. But somehow, just having her here gave Jessica an added dose of encouragement.

Jessica slipped into the open chair on the aisle of the second row. Anita sat just behind her on the third row and leaned forward, placing her hand as light as a snowflake on Jessica's shoulder. The gentle touch reassured Jessica in a simple way she hadn't felt since her mother died two Christmases ago.

As she sat down, Jessica opened the folder she'd brought with her. She decided to waste no time reviewing her notes. She wasn't concerned with anything else going on at this meeting—only that she was prepared when her time to speak came.

She read each of the bullet points carefully, then as she flipped the page to look at some additional notes she'd written on the back, she became aware that something changed.

Specifically, her nose became aware.

Jessica smelled a blend of pine and sandalwood and turned her head toward the source of the spicy, clean notes.

"You ready?" Bradley Thorpe gave her a slight elbow to the forearm as he sat down.

She tried to control her surprise at Bradley sitting next to her as she turned the paper full of typed and handwritten notes back and forth. "I hope so. I couldn't sleep last night, so I started writing everything down in a brain dump."

"That's good. Get it all out there and organized, then just review and remember." He smiled, and his teeth were as white and straight as the neat rows of twinkle lights she'd hung in the windows of Bretton's last week.

"It's kind of like preparing for a big presentation in college or studying for the final exam. I didn't think I'd be going back to that again. Even thinking about those memories makes me nervous."

Bradley laid his hand on Jessica's thigh, just above the knee and gave a squeeze. His palm rested there warmly. Jessica's gut instinct told her to twitch or adjust her position or something.

But then, something in the very back corner of her mind told her to stop, to just stay still.

She liked having the steady reassurance.

She liked having someone she trusted sitting next to her. Outside of Anita's friendship and mentorship, she hadn't experienced anything close to that since her mother died. Jessica knew no one could ever replace that kind of steady support—but for this moment, for right now—she wanted to remember how nice it used to be to have someone unconditionally in her corner.

Sure, Bradley's support would come to an end once this meeting was over—kind of like Cinderella and her pumpkin at midnight—but in the absence of the mother she'd loved so dearly, Jessica decided she'd take any semblance of a fairy godmother.

Jessica took a deep breath to calm herself as the meeting got underway. The pine and sandalwood next to her tickled her throat, but the mellow spiciness definitely made all the *what if?* thoughts in her mind settle down.

During a brief break in the discussion between the council members, Bradley leaned over and whispered in her ear. "It's almost your turn. When they tell you that you can't do it, tell them you're doing it anyway."

Jessica turned her head slightly, trying not to attract attention. She didn't understand—Bradley had made it very clear yesterday that giving her advice would be a conflict of interest. Why was he giving her advice now—and why this advice? If that wasn't a tip that could get him in trouble at his job, she didn't know what would qualify.

"I don't understand," she whispered back with a confused hiss.

"I know how to make this work."

Now she began to get nervous. Not only did her notes not say anything close to what Bradley was telling her to do, no one had ever accused her of being confrontational. Much less in front of Port Provident's mayor and all the major elected officials.

"I don't," she said simply, shaking the paper in her hand.

Bradley plucked the paper out of Jessica's hands. "Can you trust me?"

Her jaw softened. She flashed back to an almost imperceptible squeeze of the hand in a hospital room on Christmas Eve two years ago. In a voice she could barely hear over the machines, Linda Bretton left Jessica with a set of parting words that would stay with her through all the days to come.

"Trust me," Linda had said. "The person beside you may not look like me. Their voice may not sound like mine. But when you need someone, God will send you the right person at the right time. And when they speak, that's how you know I'll be right there."

Jessica looked upwards, wishing she could see all the way to Heaven instead of the ornate plaster of the ceiling in the council chambers.

A lump formed in her throat. She tried to swallow past it.

"Jessica?" Bradley tapped her leg. "They just called your name. It's your turn. Don't worry. Just be bold. I'm right behind you on this one."

For the first time since that most difficult holiday season, Jessica felt a mantle of hope settle on her shoulders like the wrap of a Christmas tree skirt. She finally knew what her mother had been talking about.

Jessica walked deliberately to the podium, standing directly across from the mayor. She took a deep breath, remembering the tingle of breathing in Bradley's cologne. Her mother had been there as she sat on the second row.

Thank you, God. The right person at the right time. She whispered the shortest prayer of thanksgiving, then reached forward and flipped the switch on the microphone.

She remembered the story of the star over Bethlehem so long ago and filled her mind with the visual. It was her time to shine brightly. She hoped she was up to the challenge.

"Hello, Mayor Ruiz. Hello, City Council members. My name is Jessica Bretton, and I own Bretton's on the Boardwalk on Harborview Drive."

Bradley sat on the edge of the uncomfortable chair. He'd sat through hundreds of City Council meetings—maybe thousands—but never had he found himself gripping the underside of the chair and leaning forward like his life depended upon it.

But maybe this time it did.

His professional life lay in ruins, thanks to some consultants who didn't know anything about him or his job.

His personal life wasn't any better. At least Jessica hadn't flinched when he patted her knee. He'd only meant for it to be a friendly gesture of reassurance, but he knew she could have viewed it as something negative.

Bradley heard Jessica take a steadying breath as she continued. "It is my understanding that the Council has canceled the Santas on the Street event this year."

Every head on the dais nodded.

"We have," said Carter. His voice fell without emotion on the microphone in front of him.

Bradley couldn't get a read on Carter. Did he sound flat because of their earlier conversation? Was he just tired of talking about Santas on the Street? Or was he completely uninterested in what Jessica had to say?

"We've always had a tourist-focused economy. We depend on others to come visit the island and generate revenue. The winter months are always tough because people don't organically come here to visit the beach. Business owners like me depend on the big, well-known events that the city has a hand in to help bring crowds. Santas on the Street has long been one of those events. I've come today with several other local business owners to ask you to reconsider."

Jessica gestured toward Beth from Café Provident and a few other small-business owners sitting near her.

Bradley couldn't quite tell what Jessica's strategy was. The last time they'd discussed it, she accepted why Santas on the Street couldn't go on. He thought she'd be fully focused on her Victorian Christmas idea.

Angela Ruiz leaned toward her mic. "We know a lot of people—tourists and locals alike—look forward to Santas on the Street every year. But Hurricane Hope has changed everything. We just can't afford to staff an event like Santas, and we can't risk the type of rowdy crowd it's generally known for."

Jessica looked down and shuffled her notes. "Would the city be able to hold a more family-friendly event?"

The mayor locked her eyes on Jessica. "What do you mean?"

Bradley saw Jessica's head straighten up.

She shuffled her notes. "A century ago, Port Provident was known for a Victorian Christmas celebration that featured the play A Christmas Carol, and other traditional things like wassail and caroling and chestnuts roasting on an open fire. All the things we hear of in stories and songs—they were here in Port Provident. They were at the heart of a Christmas celebration for the entire community. And as it grew, people came from Houston and beyond. I think something like this would be the perfect event this year."

Carter spoke again. "I don't understand. We don't have the staff to do something old or new."

"I think you'll find that it won't be a burden on the city. I have a number of local businesses who are ready to do their part. We all need a spark this holiday season."

Bradley had heard this tone of Carter's before. Carter tended to make up his mind quickly and be unchangeable. It made him a formidable opponent on Council.

It also made him sort of a jerk sometimes.

Surprisingly, Bradley realized he was holding his breath, waiting to see if Jessica would back down. He wouldn't blame her if she did. It was hard to have all those eyes staring down on you. Many, many times over the years, he'd been behind that same microphone where Jessica now stood.

"Ms. Bretton, I'm sorry, but I don't know how we could do anything like what you're describing. This Christmas season will have to be low-key this year. Next year, you're welcome to come to our planning session in the summer and submit your idea. We'll certainly consider it."

Bradley began to stand up. He owned that meeting. Surely it wouldn't be inappropriate for him to say something.

But just then, Jessica's shoulders pushed back and leveled out. He saw her shift her weight on her feet and stand a little taller.

"Sitting around and waiting is not what Port Provident has ever been about. I won't need to be at that meeting next summer because I will not have a business to represent then. Without intervention now, I will be closing my doors in the new year. Your Christmas may need to be low-key, Councilman, but Bretton's on the Boardwalk has been in the business of holiday cheer for a century. I believe there's more that can be done."

With that, she turned and walked back to her seat.

Carter's voice followed Jessica back down the aisle. "You're welcome to do something individually at your own business, but Ms. Bretton, be aware that you will be responsible for everything— including security. The city cannot and will not be supporting this."

"I understand," she said as she took her seat. The edge to her whisper could have cut an ice cube in half.

She crossed her legs at the knee. Bradley wanted to reach out one more time. He wanted to give her a pat of reassurance.

But he stopped himself.

Jessica Bretton needed a solution. Not a crush from a guy who didn't have much of a future in Port Provident. She needed to believe in something. He wasn't that guy…not anymore.

3

———

"**C**ome on, we're going to dinner. We've got to plan." Bradley wanted to take Jessica's shoulders and hug the self-conscious slump out of them.

He jogged across two rows of the parking lot and met Jessica before she climbed into her little red hatchback.

"I really just need to get back to the store, Bradley. I don't know what I thought I could accomplish in there. We all have passion, but we're just small businesses. Emphasis on the small."

"No, you don't need to go back to your store, Jessica," he said matter-of-factly. "You need to *save* your store."

"I just need to accept the inevitable. I need to make plans to close my store. You heard them. They won't do anything to save local businesses right now. There's no saving Bretton's." She tucked a stray blonde curl behind her ear.

Jessica had been bold in there, but she'd remained respectful—as he'd known she would. She'd followed his advice as best she could, but her sweet disposition wasn't going to allow her to push back as hard as she'd needed to. He'd formulated his plan based on how he would have responded. He hadn't had time to tweak it for her more gentle personality.

But he hadn't given her his advice just because sitting in that room right beside her, feeling both her nervousness and the way his hand cupped her knee perfectly had made him remember the crush he'd tried to keep in check for a year.

He'd more given the advice for himself. If they were going to turn him into a party planner, he was going to plan the biggest and best party the island had ever seen. And do it without breaking the crazy rules that covered the city right now.

Getting to plan it beside Jessica Bretton's side would just be a bonus.

"I don't understand what you're thinking, though," Jessica said.

Bradley smiled again. "Come to dinner with me, and you'll find out. There is a way to make this happen."

Jessica looked at her watch. "Dinner? It's four-thirty in the afternoon."

"I didn't get lunch." He jingled the keys to his truck. "Come on— I'll even give you a ride *and* let you call the meal lunch or dinner or whatever name you want."

She turned and walked toward the truck, shoulders still weighed down with the defeat of her proposal by the City Council. "Okay."

He opened the door for Jessica, then closed it behind her. She deserved the royal treatment anyway, but especially now. He would lighten her load any way he could today. "Let's get to Porter's, and I'll lay everything out for you."

Jessica wasn't in a chatting mood, but Bradley coaxed her out of her shell by making small talk for the few blocks it took to drive from the city government building to Gulfview Boulevard and Porter's Seafood, a Port Provident institution for almost as long as Bretton's had been in business.

"I've lived here my whole life—but I still don't think I'll ever get tired of looking at the waves," Jessica said as she stole a glance at the surf crashing upon the sand.

"I couldn't agree more, although I haven't lived here nearly that long." Bradley turned into a parking space near the door. "I hope they have a table available by the window."

Once they were seated and had placed their order, Bradley turned the conversation back to the day's events. "Do you have any more paper in that folder? I might need to take some notes."

"Sure." Jessica pulled out several sheets of plain white paper and a pen. "Will this do?"

"Perfect."

Bradley pushed the loaf of warm bread to the edge of the table and laid the pen and paper in the center of the white tablecloth.

"Here's what you're going to need to do. I saw the number of people there today supporting you. It seems like a number of downtown businesses want to take part in this."

Jessica took a sip of iced tea, then placed the glass back in the corner. "They do. Everyone I've talked to has been enthusiastic about the idea."

"Well, that's good because everyone is going to have to work together. If you all have small events in your own businesses on the same day at the same time with the same theme, they can't stop you. There aren't permits needed for that kind of thing."

Pulling the paper closer, Bradley began to write down the names of the different stores that could get involved and then matched them with ideas.

"Look here—Café Provident can serve wassail and roasted chestnuts. Bretton's can host photos with Queen Victoria and Santa Claus and Tiny Tim. Betsy's Boutique can have a choir singing. The Port Provident T-shirt Company can host a reading of A Christmas Carol. The theatre can perform it a couple of times that day. Do you see what I'm saying? These are all off the top of my head—you'll probably want to refine them, but if each business hosts something unique, then tourists can walk from one business to the next and get a fulfilling experience."

Bradley watched Jessica's eyes scan the notes he'd scribbled on the page.

"But how will they know? How will we make sure everyone gets from place to place?"

"There can be maps and a list in every store. Maybe some kind of card they can get punched for some kind of prize or gift at the end? That will help make sure everyone goes inside of each location."

Slowly, a smile began to cross Jessica's face. "So... if we coordinate, we won't need a permit?"

"Right. You don't have to ask the city's permission to hold a sale in your store or to have a special event like a cookbook signing, do you?"

She shook her head. "Well, no."

"Same thing. A ton of this city's event permits come to my desk in some form or fashion. I have a defined scope of things that I can approve without going back to City Council. As long as we keep things within those parameters, I'll greenlight other ideas, too."

"You'd do that for me?"

Bradley wanted to say yes, he'd do it for her—that he was doing this all for her—but he couldn't. She'd made it clear that she didn't think of him as anything more than a friend, as someone she had a very cordial working relationship with.

It would be wrong of him to do anything that didn't respect the signals she'd given.

But just as much as he could see the flicker of hope in her eyes as she pieced together the small threads that would come together to revitalize Port Provident's tradition of a Victorian Christmas, he couldn't help but wish that just once, he could see that same flicker in her eyes because of him.

Jessica knew she wouldn't sleep much tonight. The longer she and Bradley brainstormed about how to pull off the Victorian Christmas celebration, the more excited she became. This was going to become a reality—and it had the potential to be even better than she'd ever hoped or dreamed.

If she could just get enough momentum to stay afloat until Spring Break, when beach-loving tourists returned to the island, then she might keep Bretton's doors open.

"Do you mind if I make a stop on the way back to dropping you off at your car?"

"After everything you've done for me today? Absolutely not. I'm not in a rush—even if I went back to the store, my mind is racing so much I don't think I could focus on anything. I'd probably start giving people the wrong change back or something." She gave a dry laugh. "And I really can't afford that these days. You're probably doing me a favor by keeping Donna behind the counter instead of me."

Bradley turned at the stoplight, then drove a few blocks and pulled up in the circle in front of one of the island's oldest churches, First Central Church of Port Provident—known to locals as First Provident.

"You can come in if you'd like. I just need to drop off a camel harness. You don't have to wait in the car," he said.

Jessica's first instinct was to wave off the invitation. But then she realized she had too much energy flowing through her veins to sit still and alone in the car. Maybe if she walked off a little of this idea-induced adrenaline, she could settle down and get focused.

"Camel harness?" She reached for the door handle.

"This is where I go to church. I'm helping out behind the scenes with the live nativity this year." Bradley reached out and touched her left hand. "Just stay put. I'll get that."

He got out, walked around the front of the truck and opened the door.

"Really, you don't have to do that. I can get my own door."

He nodded. "I'm sure you can. You're a very capable woman who runs her own business. But you shouldn't have to. My mom's been in Heaven for fifteen years, but no amount of time will ever erase the sound of her voice in my ear, telling me what behavior was expected of me."

Jessica placed one foot gingerly on the running board and the other on the concrete below. "My mom's been gone for two years. Sometimes, I worry that I'm forgetting the sound of her voice in my ear."

Bradley seemed to hesitate, then lightly squeezed Jessica's

shoulder. Instead of feeling uneasy and trying to duck the friendly gesture, Jessica surprised herself as the corners of her mouth turned up to a small smile.

"I didn't know your mom had passed away," she said quietly as they walked up the stairs to the front door of the red brick building with the tall white steeple on top.

"Yeah. She was working New Year's at a restaurant in Houston, and a drunk driver hit her on the way home from her shift. He walked away from the accident with two bruised ribs and a cut on his head that required three stitches. She didn't even make it through the doors of the hospital with a pulse. It changes things. It makes you remember the things they said, especially the ones that didn't seem so important at the time."

Jessica felt a shake inside. "It changes everything. My dad had trouble coping with losing her and said he needed to get away. He turned the store over to me and went to Florida. In the space of three months, it was like I lost them both."

"Have you talked to him about what's going on at the store?"

Guilt washed over her with the glare of a spotlight finding a target. "No."

She could barely get the one word out.

"Do you think you should?"

She couldn't tell him how many times she'd asked herself the same question as she listened to the silence inside of Bretton's the last month or so. But in the end, she'd always come to the same conclusion.

"It wouldn't change anything one way or the other. He's started a new life. I don't think he wants to be reminded of this old one he's left behind."

The sound of her mother's voice had started to fade with time. But so had the sound of her dad's. He hadn't called in months. And Jessica hadn't picked up the phone, either, because she didn't know how to start a conversation with someone that had left when she needed him the most.

Bradley cupped her shoulder and gave it one more squeeze. He didn't say anything—he just let her know he was there. Jessica hadn't felt like anyone had been there for her the last two years.

She lifted her head and walked into the church, wondering if—like a present—there had been more to Bradley Thorpe than she'd let herself see. She'd considered him a friend for a while now, but had she only seen the wrapping paper and not the substance underneath?

Jessica watched as Bradley walked down the hall to the choir rehearsal room. She didn't quite see the connection between musical numbers and camels, but it was possible that she was too filled with stress about the store and ideas for the Victorian Christmas to fully appreciate the situation.

As external evidence of all her tossed-up internal feelings, Jessica began to pace near one of the front windows, lost in thoughts of the City Council meeting and the meal with Bradley.

And she also couldn't stop thinking about the way he'd gently reassured her more than once today, when she needed it most.

"Jessica, honey, you're going to wear a hole in that carpet. Even Hurricane Hope didn't do that kind of damage in here."

Jessica turned her head slowly upwards and saw Diana Peoples, Port Provident's unofficial matriarch. If Diana had been sitting on that City Council dais earlier, she wouldn't have left Jessica hanging. No one cared more for the people, the history, and the traditions of Port Provident than Diana Peoples.

All of a sudden, Jessica's feet came to a complete stop.

The thought recycled in her mind. No one cared more for the people, the history, and the traditions of Port Provident than Diana Peoples.

Diana would know what to do.

"I'm sorry, Diana." Jessica fumbled over the apology as she tried to figure out how to approach the older lady.

"You don't need to apologize to me, Jessica—or even the floor. I can tell something's wrong. What's going on?"

Just like that, Jessica felt a door opening. Diana had asked. Jessica needed to answer honestly and not give some well-meaning platitude, like she usually did. This wasn't a time for small talk.

Small talk could only lead to small action.

And saving Bretton's would require big action.

"It's the store." Jessica put it directly out there. She knew she needed to say more, but this would give her a start as she searched for the best way to describe things to Diana.

Diana nodded thoughtfully. "Well, it's almost Christmas. And that should be the best time of the year for Bretton's, right? Things should come together soon."

Jessica shook her head and held her breath. She could feel a few wayward tears pricking at her eyes. Diana didn't see what was going on, either. Perhaps she wouldn't be able to help Jessica and the other business owners after all.

Diana looked at Jessica with a quizzical expression. "Is something going on?"

"The tourists. They're not coming. They're not buying. And the City Council just canceled Santas on the Street for this year. There's nothing to get people down here to buy. And without customers…" Jessica let out a sigh. "Well, you know what that means."

This time, Diana's nod was slow and measured. "I absolutely do. Makes it hard to pay the bills, doesn't it?"

Relief washed over Jessica like one of Hurricane Hope's waves. She couldn't talk to her dad about this, but she could talk to Diana— and that was close enough for now. Diana got it. And Jessica felt the power of that knowledge deep in her bones. If she could convert the formidable Diana Powell Peoples to become an ally for the downtown merchants, then maybe…just maybe…

"It does," Jessica answered.

Diana jumped in with a question before Jessica could continue. "Is it just your store, or are there others feeling this slow down?"

Now was her chance to advocate for the entire downtown district. "It's all of us. It's not that people aren't buying for Christmas. It's that they think Port Provident is still shuttered and down because of the hurricane. They're still celebrating the season and spending their money, but they're doing it on the mainland and in other places."

"Didn't Mayor Ruiz just go on TV in Houston and the other major Texas cities? Wasn't she talking about how well the recovery is going?"

"Yes, she did. She's been everywhere the past few weeks," Jessica acknowledged.

"So maybe just a little more time is what we need?"

Jessica could feel the icicles of fear again. They snaked through her veins every time she thought about closing Bretton's doors for the last time.

And she thought about that final turn of the key in the lock often.

Too often.

"I wish it was that simple. But I'm hurting. Badly. Café Provident is hurting. The theatre is hurting. It's everyone in every business type across the board. And with several months of income literally washed away by the hurricane, we just cannot afford a soft holiday season. The news says this will be one of the biggest Christmas buying seasons on record, but we aren't seeing it. And it's killing us."

Diana placed her purse in a nearby wingback chair. "Have you talked to Angela Ruiz? She's going to be a great mayor. She cares about this city and the recovery. Deeply. I'm so glad she's leading the way for us now."

"I spoke at today's City Council meeting. I laid out some ideas that our group had."

Jessica saw a light in Diana's eyes. "Wonderful. What did they say?"

"That we were on our own. There's no budget to provide city services for anything extra right now."

"I can understand that." Diana leaned over and dug in her purse. She pulled out a small notepad and a pen. "But I also understand that the situation you're describing is just as critical to the long-term health of our city. So, what were your ideas?"

For the second time today, Jessica stated her case. She'd left her notes in Bradley's truck, but this time, she didn't need them. Bradley had given her so many ideas and so much inspiration while they dined at Porter's.

This time, Jessica spoke from the heart. She talked with her hands. She over-explained. She connected the dots.

And when she finished, a smile crested on Diana's face.

"Is that all?"

Jessica almost felt out of breath. She'd just pulled off a marathon. "Basically."

"I like it," Diana said as she closed her notepad. "You know, my dear, I've always wanted to be Mrs. Claus. I'm meeting Jake and Gracie and the grandbabies for movie night at their house, so I have to run. But let's talk more about this soon, okay?"

Jessica felt the line of her eyebrows squish together. She didn't quite understand where the older woman was going with that. If she was honest, Diana's initial reaction disappointed Jessica.

She hated to admit it, but she'd been hoping for something like a big check to pull it all together. Not just some ho-ho-hos and an offer to chat more later.

They could definitely find a place for Diana to take part, and just having her involvement would mean something.

But nothing meant more than cold, hard cash.

Talking more later would be too late. She needed some forward motion now.

Something deep and sticky pooled down in Jessica's belly. Loathing, pure and simple. That was it. It pulled Jessica down.

Moments before, she'd been so excited to share her ideas with Diana.

And now, she felt as though she'd been slapped back down.

She hated this feeling. She hated that instead of seeing Diana for the amazing woman she was, Jessica had chosen to pin her hopes not on Diana the person, but Diana the checkbook.

Jessica had been raised on Christmas. And she'd hoped that *A Christmas Carol* would be the key to saving her store. But now, all she felt like was Scrooge.

The loss she'd gone through the last two years—culminating in the current struggle after Hurricane Hope—had turned Jessica into someone she didn't recognize or want to be.

4

———

On Monday, Jessica answered her phone on the first ring. She'd been staring at the screen for almost an hour, absently scrolling through social media. Following the lives of friends and strangers alike made it easier to not think about her own life.

"I think I've got some news you're going to like."

The voice on the other end of the line belonged to Bradley.

"Do tell."

"I've got you an interview with Channel Four to talk about Victorian Christmas on their morning show. They're going to come down here and film you live on the square."

Visions of stuttering and turning into a red-faced mess on live television danced in Jessica's head. "Wait, what? I can't be on TV."

"Sure you can. You've done commercials for the store before. I've seen them."

Jessica flashed back to her childhood. Every year, her parents dressed her up in a smocked dress and had her do a commercial for local TV. When she took over the store, she stopped the tradition.

"I am not wearing an embroidered Peter Pan collar on Good Morning Gulf Coast."

Bradley laughed. "I'm sure some antlers or a red nose would do just fine."

"Bradley. Stop." Jessica didn't know whether to be embarrassed or amused. "How did this come about?

"I had some business at the CVB today. One of their reporters was there. I asked."

"It was that simple to get us a morning show live spot on the highest-rated morning news show in the region?"

"Well, it is when people like you." Bradley laid the smug tone on thick.

This time, it was Jessica's turn to laugh. "Oh, they do, do they?"

"You do," he hit back without so much as a second's pause.

"Well…I mean…"

He cut off her attempt to explain away his assertion. "Not like that."

Jessica wished she felt as confident about it as he sounded. But then she remembered how he'd reassuringly put his hand on her knee before she stepped up to talk to City Council. She remembered that she didn't push it away.

But she wasn't about to tell him that. He'd been a good friend. And good friends helped. He'd helped her then and he was helping her now. She didn't need to make any of it out to be something it wasn't.

"Okay, so give me details."

Bradley gave her the specifics, but before they could wrap up the conversation, a beep sounded.

"Hey, that's my other line," Bradley said. "I need to grab this. It's Eddie down at the Pocket Park. I'll catch up with you about it soon, okay?"

"Okay," Jessica answered as he disconnected.

Jessica couldn't have asked for a better friend the last few days as she navigated how to save Bretton's. But when the season was over, she assumed they'd go back to being friendly people who crossed paths from time to time.

And the thought of that seemed as disappointing as a lump of coal in her stocking.

~

"You just missed Jessica!" Beth Greenling grabbed Bradley by the shoulders and pulled him into a tight hug.

He didn't know what was going on here, but it was a nice departure from the day he came by to take down the Santas on the Street poster and thought he was in danger of a rogue barista spitting into his coffee.

Today, everyone was sunshine and smiles—a nice feeling for the first week in December, when a bit of a chill began to slip into the air.

"I'll try and catch up with her later."

"She was so excited," Beth gushed. "She said you've gotten Channel Four to come down and do a TV interview with us!"

Bradley let a smile slip across his face. Beth's enthusiasm was contagious.

"I had a chance to talk with them today. But she didn't seem quite so excited about doing the interview."

Beth waved a hand dismissively. "She's not a social butterfly. But she'll do fine. She asked me if I would do the interview, but I very firmly told her no. This project is her baby—even though I think we all are becoming very passionate about it. There will be plenty of people there to support her. I'll start asking some others in the community to come out, as well. We'll make it as easy on her as we can. Now, what can we do for you?"

"Coffee. I just need some coffee. I've been in meetings since nine o'clock this morning and my head is screaming for some caffeine." Bradley placed the thick file folder he brought with him on the closest table.

"We can do that. Black, right?"

Bradley nodded. "Plain and simple. Just like me."

Beth swatted at him with a white dishtowel. "I don't believe that for a second. Lilly! Can you get Mr. Tall, Dark, and Handsome here a tall black?"

A head popped up from behind the counter. "I don't see anyone fitting that description."

Bradley recognized the blonde barista as one of the two who'd been upset by the cancellation of Santas on the Street. This time, he reminded himself to check the cup—just to be on the safe side.

"*Pfft*. You know Bradley from the Park Board."

Lilly smirked slightly. "Santa killer," she said, almost under her breath—but not quite.

"Whaaaat?" Beth asked her employee.

"He's the one who canceled Santas on the Street." Lilly's voice was flatter than the flattest flat white.

Bradley felt his spine stiffen. "I didn't cancel it. I just had to do the dirty work."

Beth leapt in the conversation. "He's also the one who helped Jess get Victorian Christmas off the ground. That means all is forgiven. I think Victorian Christmas is going to be bigger with families than Santas on the Street ever was. I truly believe this will be a blessing for the whole island."

Lilly handed the insulated paper cup to Bradley. "So… you're working with Jessica?"

"I am."

Maybe he wasn't quite skating on thin ice anymore. But until he was certain, Bradley wasn't giving Lilly—or her side-eye—anything but the minimum number of syllables.

"Okay. Then maybe you're okay."

Bradley gave a half-shrug. That was probably the highest praise he'd ever get from Lilly. He'd take it.

"Which way did Jessica go?"

Beth handed him a napkin. "She said she was going to put posters in the downtown stores, so I guess she'll be around here somewhere."

Posters in stores? Bradley knew that route. He could catch up to her quickly.

He didn't know why—but since the moment Beth mentioned Jessica's name, Bradley needed to see Jessica even more than he needed the cup of coffee he came in here for in the first place.

"Sounds good—I'll see you soon."

Bradley picked up his folder off the table and headed out the door.

Even the winter wind seemed to be giving him a push down the street toward Jessica.

He spotted her about halfway down the block, taping a colorful poster to the front window of Georgia's Jewelry and Antiques. Brad decided to play it cool and stand outside, taking slow sips of his coffee.

He wasn't fooling himself.

He needed a few moments to decide what he was going to say. "Hey there, Beth told me I missed you, so I grabbed my coffee and took off down Harborview to see if I could find you" sounded really lame. Coming off with a stalker vibe wasn't going to impress her.

But being honest—that he didn't just *want* to see her, he *needed* to see her—wasn't going to sound any less creepy at this point.

He wished he could be honest about his long-harbored crush. But not now. Not while her mind was so preoccupied with Victorian Christmas and saving Bretton's. It wasn't fair to put anything else on her.

As the bell on the door jangled, Bradley took a step down the sidewalk.

"Hey! I didn't think I'd see you down here." She waved a stack of rectangular paper. "Wanna hang some posters instead of taking them down?"

Bradley took one last sip of his coffee and tossed the cup in the trash can on the sidewalk. He smiled to himself. "Don't mind if I do."

He reached out and took the stack from Jessica's hands, and they went from business to business in the downtown district. They hung posters in restaurants, clothing stores, souvenir shops, lawyer's offices, dance studios, and even an acupuncturist's practice that had recently opened.

Everyone seemed excited to have a family-friendly event to invite people to. There wasn't one among them who wasn't ready for the crowds to come back to Port Provident.

As they hung the last poster inside of Sand Dollar Dance Academy, Cara Keeler, the studio's owner, was just getting out of teaching an advanced class to a group of teenagers.

"Tonight's the perfect night to go Christmas caroling! It's finally cold." A dark-haired ballerina nudged the friend next to her.

Her friend nodded rapidly. "Squeal. Yes. Let's do it!"

Three other nearby girls came closer. "Now?"

"Yeah. Let's go. I'll just text my mom and tell here I'll be home later."

Bradley turned and looked at Jessica. She tucked her blonde hair behind one ear.

"Want to join them?" he asked.

She tucked the almost-empty roll of clear tape into the back pocket of her jeans. "It looks like we're out of posters."

"We are," Bradley confirmed.

"Then I guess we should."

Cara locked up the studio behind the group of excited girls in leotards and skirts and a hodge podge of puffy jackets and hoodies. She couldn't contain her own set of giggles. "What should we sing first?"

The first teenager in line raised her hand and gave a little jump. "Oh, I know! How about *Here Comes Santa Claus*?"

She quickly received a high-five. "Love it."

And suddenly, the group took off down the street singing the familiar tune.

Bradley and Jessica brought up the rear. As Jessica started to sing, Bradley couldn't believe how off-key Jessica's voice sounded. She had crystal blue eyes, long blonde hair, and a killer figure. For some reason, it had never occurred to him that she wasn't the perfect crush in every way.

But, he decided, her funky warble made him like her even more.

Jessica caught him staring. "I was asked to leave the children's choir at church when I was six. True story."

"Really?" The image made him laugh, even though he knew that had to be the wrong action to take.

She nodded, a wide grin appearing on her faith. "Scout's honor. I'm the only Christmas elf who can't sing."

"Surely you're not the only one."

She raised her hands as she shrugged. "All evidence to the contrary."

"Well, maybe if we can get some more people to join us, they can drown you out." Bradley paused instantly. Where was his filter? He shouldn't have said that.

He began to apologize, but before he could get the words out, Jessica started laughing. Then she doubled over and stopped walking. As soon as she caught her breath, she ran up to the door of the Provident Youth Theatre and threw it open. She ran inside, then came out just a few moments later.

"They're rehearsing for *A Christmas Carol*, but they're coming. I think there are about twenty of them. Do you think that's enough to do the trick?"

Bradley shook his head. "I'm not touching that with a ten-foot candy cane. There's no correct answer to it."

The smile she gave him would have melted a snowman's heart. It turned Bradley's into a puddle instantly. "You're probably right. But I bet it's a good start."

The street had been lined with garlands intertwined with twinkle lights, and the small glow caught the edge of Jessica's eyes as she looked up at Bradley while they sang *It Came Upon a Midnight Clear*. She gave him a warm smile—just the corners of her mouth upturned, no teeth showing—and reached for his hand.

"Come on, you're slowing down. We need to catch up."

Bradley felt the curves of her hand slide across his palm. Jessica gave a gentle squeeze, then tugged him forward to catch up with the group. She didn't let go.

He knew he would hold her hand as long as she wanted.

He'd have followed her anywhere right then.

Even to the North Pole.

The next morning, Jessica dropped off the last of the posters at the Port Provident Historical Society. Her best friend, Samantha Spaeth, was the director of the organization. She told Jessica she had some volunteers who needed materials to help spread the word.

Jessica felt immense gratitude for anyone who wanted to put time and effort behind getting more attendees for the Victorian Christmas celebration. Anything she could do to help them help out—it was time well spent in Jessica's book.

Time with Samantha was also quality time in Jessica's book. Demands on Samantha's calendar had shot through the roof this past year. She'd opened a new tourist attraction dedicated to the Great Storm of 1910. It focused on the lives lost at the Port Provident Children's Home, one of the most poignant stories of all those that came out of the storm. She'd also been a part of a special that aired on Home and Hearth network. On top of all that, she'd met the man of her dreams last Christmas and she and Whitt Peoples—Diana's grandson —were planning their own happily-ever-after.

Jessica felt so much happiness for her friend.

But at the same time, it made her feel a little empty.

"These posters will be perfect. I'm headed over to Provident College today to speak in one of the history classes. I'll hang some up while I'm there." Samantha looked at the illustration on the oversized paper with a fond smile. "Who did the design on these? I've got some upcoming projects for the spring that I could use some help on."

"Actually, Bradley put them together. He said the graphic designer for the tourism team is still living off the island, so she's only working part-time."

Samantha laughed. "Bradley Thorpe. Is there anything he can't do these days?"

Jessica fell into uncharacteristic silence. Usually she always had a quip or retort for her best friend. But right now? Nope. She had nothing.

"Cat got your tongue?" Samantha's eyes locked on Jessica's face, searching her expression like a missile focusing in on a target.

Without even thinking about it, Jessica took a step back. Samantha had read her like one of the brochures lined up along the counter. But Jessica didn't really want to answer Samantha's question.

As she thought about it, though, she realized it was more that she couldn't think of anything Bradley couldn't do. He'd pretty much done it all during the last few weeks.

Lightning-quick, a memory from last night flashed into Jessica's mind.

Samantha raised her eyebrows. "Spill it."

"What?" Jessica tried to protest, but it quickly became evident that Samantha saw right through her.

"Brad. Ley. Thorpe." Samantha laid down the posters and crossed her arms, as if speaking in individual syllables didn't call Jessica out enough. "You're holding something back. Spill it."

The only thing Jessica wanted to hold was Bradley's hand. Again.

But could she really tell Samantha? Sam would think she was crazy.

"Bradley's just a nice guy, that's all. Helpful." Jessica decided to stick to the most basic levels of truth.

Samantha pursed her lips. "*Mmmhmm*. I know that. I also know that's not at all what you're thinking about. I've known you how long?"

"Like ten years." Jessica answered this question quickly, grateful to move the conversation away from Bradley. Maybe she could keep steering it in another direction.

"Exactly. So spill it." She gave Jessica *that* stare again. "Look, if you can't tell me, who can you tell? Bradley?"

Jessica felt heat rush to her cheeks. They probably were as bright as Rudolph's nose. "Ugh. No! I can't tell him."

"Good." Samantha put her hands on her hips. "That just leaves me."

"Fine." If Jessica didn't start talking, her best friend would probably bar the door so she couldn't leave. And at some point, Donna would need a lunch break over at Bretton's, so Jessica decided she'd better come clean now so she could leave later. "Last night while we were all out caroling, I grabbed his hand—you know, to pull him along because he was falling behind—but I realized I didn't want to let go. So, I didn't."

"And?" Samantha stretched out the question like the saltwater taffy they made over at Island Confectionary.

"He didn't either."

"And?" Samantha did it again.

The heat from her cheeks began to spread. Jessica could feel it inching toward her hairline. "Why are you tormenting me?"

Samantha let out a whoop, then grabbed Jessica with a strong hug. "Because Bradley Thorpe has had a crush on you for I don't even know how long. I've been waiting for you to see it. Whitt and I think he's perfect for you."

Jessica felt something akin to whiplash inside as she pulled back from the hug. "Wait. What? You and Whitt have been talking about me?"

"We have dinner with you every few weeks. Of course we talk about you." Samantha smiled, and the corners of her eyes crinkled slightly. "All good things. You're the best friend I've got. We want only the best for you. I want you to be as happy as I've been this last year—and Whitt does too."

"But Bradley?" Jessica struggled to get out anything coherent.

"Yes, Bradley."

"But how? I can't just come out and tell him I think I like him. That would sound ridiculous. And we're working together on the Victorian Christmas project. I cannot mess up Victorian Christmas, Samantha. I can't take the risk."

Samantha's smile mellowed. The warmth radiated from her like a low flicker in a fireplace. "I understand. But having someone beside you for life is one of those things that's worth the risk. Whitt gave up his career and everything back in New York so he could get to know me—and his family—better. It was worth it. When the circumstances are right, you'll know. And when they are, just go with it, okay? Take a risk on yourself, Jessica. I promise you're worth it too, my friend."

"Are you ever going to work out front again?" Bradley stood in the doorway to Jessica's office in the stockroom at Bretton's. "I've stopped by three times in the last two days, and each time, Donna's said you're holed up back here like a hermit. I heard someone say they're going to rename this place "Donna's" since she's the only person ever around now."

Jessica looked up and gave him a playful scowl. "Hush it."

"Now there's the Christmas spirit." He couldn't keep from smiling at her. She had pulled her long, honey-golden hair into a makeshift bun on the top of her head and stabbed a pencil through it to hold it in place. She had no makeup on, and her only accessory was a pair of glasses with a thin black frame snaking across the top of the two lenses.

He'd carried his crush on her in his back pocket for far too long, but in all that time, he didn't think he'd ever seen her look more beautiful.

"I'm pulling you out of this Hobbit workroom. You're taking a break."

"I can't, Bradley. Tomorrow is the interview with the TV station from Houston. I've got to be ready."

Bradley walked across the room and stood behind her chair, then tugged it away from her desk. "Do you know how many interviews I've done with Channel Four? You're coming to lunch with me. You can call it media training or coaching, or whatever you want. But you're taking a break."

She held up papers covered in sticky notes. "Do you see all this? I can't."

"I see it." He tugged at the papers in her right hand and placed them on the desk. Then he tugged at the papers in her left hand and did the same. "Don't care. Come on. You're going to burn yourself out and be worthless on TV tomorrow and for the event itself."

He put his hand on her back and guided her out of the chair and the back office.

"I'm going for a quick lunch, Donna," she said as they passed the front counter. "Under duress. If anyone asks, tell them I've been kidnapped."

Bradley shook his head and laughed. "Don't bother. I know the mayor."

"Name dropper." Sarcasm dripped from Jessica's words like hot grease of a freshly-cooked French fry.

"Whatever it takes." He pointed toward the parking lot at the end of the block. "My truck's in that lot. Come on."

Bradley drove through a fast food restaurant and picked up the basics of burgers and fries, then headed out the Open Water Highway to the tip of the island. They passed through the gate of the Point Provident Beach Park, and Bradley took his city-issued truck straight out onto the sand.

"I didn't know you could drive out on the sand," Jessica said as Bradley stopped the truck at the edge of the surf.

He laughed a little to himself. "Precisely why I brought you out here. *You* can't drive on the sand, but *I* can. A perk of the job. At least for now."

She poked a straw through the lid of her drink. "What do you mean?"

"My job is changing." Bradley tried to stay neutral in his words. "They're merging the Park Board with the Convention and Visitors Bureau due to some requirements for Hurricane Hope recovery funds. They haven't completely explained to me what it means for my job, but there's not a whole lot I can do about it."

Jessica turned away from looking at the water and looked straight at Bradley. He could feel the softness of her stare. "Wait a minute. When did they tell you about this?"

"Carter Porter pulled me aside before the City Council meeting the other day."

She didn't break the linear focus between them. "So that's why you decided to help me?"

"Not exactly." Bradley could feel something in this conversation begin to tug at him, like the edges of an undertow. If he didn't watch out, he'd get dragged under.

"Well, one minute you were swearing up and down you couldn't help me and then the next time I saw you, you told me to call the mayor's bluff. It looks to me like you were trying to get them back or something."

Bradley finished a handful of French fries before answering. "In truth, Jess, there may have been a little of that there. I can't say I'm not frustrated with the turn of events. What I do is very different than what the CVB does, and I'm not comfortable with them having oversight of my department and me. But that's not the real reason I sat next to you at the council meeting."

She raised an eyebrow. "So, what was it?"

He looked out the front windshield of the car, weighing his options. If he came clean now, there was no going back.

But, if he *didn't* come clean now, though, there was no going back either—but in an entirely different way, and he didn't think he could live with that. He couldn't continue to be just friends with Jessica.

"I wanted to." It was a simple statement, but just putting it out there made Bradley's mouth go dry, in spite of the 64-ounce soda in the cup holder next to him.

Jessica put her bag of fast food on the dashboard. "Do you mind if we get out and take a walk for a second?"

The sky looked like wintery cashmere, and a steady breeze was blowing parallel to the lines of the surf. The temperature for the day would top out in the mid-40s. Bradley had lived up north and knew these weren't exactly harsh winter conditions. This was about as severe as it got on Provident Island.

It wasn't exactly "take a leisurely stroll" kind of weather, but the air today was fresh and crisp. Maybe it could clear some of the tension that had just built up in the truck.

"Hold on, I'll get the door for you." He pre-emptively waved off the sentence he knew was coming. "And no, I don't have to. I want to. You deserve a little bit of pampering right now while you're working so hard to pull the Victorian Christmas off."

She smiled sheepishly and stayed put while Bradley made his way around the truck. He had to walk around the back since the front tires were parked in the water. The short trip to the passenger side gave him a moment to collect his thoughts.

Then, as he placed his hand on the door handle, he through all of it into the gulf breeze.

He'd said what he most needed to say. What he needed to know now were Jessica's thoughts.

Bradley didn't even realize he held his breath slightly as he opened the door.

"Thanks," Jessica smiled shyly as she slid her feet carefully down to the sand.

She took a few steps down the beach. Bradley locked the truck and quickly caught up to her, watching and listening for any sign that would let him know what to do next.

They walked for a few minutes with the sound of the surf as their companion, then Jessica spoke. "I really do appreciate your help, Bradley. There wouldn't be a plan if it weren't for your encouragement and your ideas. I'd honestly have just given up after City Council told me thanks but no thanks."

"I don't believe that." Bradley spoke the truth as he saw it. "I think you're a fighter."

She stopped abruptly. "I used to think so. I don't anymore."

"Why not?" Bradley stopped one step ahead, then turned to face her.

"This last year or so…" She hesitated, then looked down at the wet sand below her feet. "I got a letter from the county not long ago that my dad didn't pay the taxes on the building downtown last year. I have to be caught up by January 1. It was always going to be tough to catch up, but then the hurricane happened, and everything fell apart. When you put it all together, the hole seems too deep. I just haven't felt like there was much to fight for. My mom isn't coming back. My dad isn't either. My family's business is about selling Christmas cheer and holiday spirit all year long. I haven't had any Christmas spirit for two years."

She looked up and her eyes brimmed with tears. "I'm a fake, Bradley. I don't take risks. I play it safe now. Every day I get up and fake it. Don't get me wrong, I *do* want to save the store. But it's because I don't want to let my family down. But what then? Every day it stays open is another day I have to pretend that I'm feeling holly and jolly."

Suddenly, that one step between them looked like a canyon. Bradley moved closer and stretched out his hands.

He hadn't fought, either. He'd bitten his tongue and hidden his feelings and tried to stay out of Jessica's way for the whole last year. In reality, she'd needed someone by her side this year more than ever before.

He realized he had a lot to fight for.

Bradley wasn't going to be silent anymore, and he wasn't going to let her feel alone one more moment.

He wrapped Jessica in his arms, folded them across her back, and pulled her tight.

He could smell a whiff of salt in the air and a casual scent of magnolia at her neck. He could hear the low roar of the surf, always rolling to shore. Then he heard the voice in his head telling him to come home, to make his move, too.

He leaned down and let the tide of the moment pull them together. When Bradley felt the soft yield of her lips and the slightly sticky touch of her lipstick, he was hooked. All that waiting and wondering about what he should say…it turns out that the proper response wasn't made of words at all.

With a light touch, Jessica lifted her arms slightly and placed her hands on Bradley's waist.

Nothing else mattered.

Except for the squawk of a nosy seagull that landed at their feet.

Jessica pulled back, startled by the throaty honk. The kiss ended, but Bradley continued to hold his hands at the small of her back. The moment still lingered.

But what words would be needed now?

"That wasn't fake, right?" He posed the question with enough sarcasm in his voice that he could laugh it off if he needed to.

Jessica looked at Bradley, then down at the seagull—who had

apparently signaled for a crowd of friends to join them. "I don't think so."

He barely heard her whisper over the sound of the nearby waves.

"Me neither," he agreed. "I didn't bring you out here to do that, Jessica. I brought you out here for a break and some fresh air. That said, I don't think I'm going to apologize for it."

"I don't want you to apologize, Bradley." She dropped her hands from his waist. "But I don't know what we do next. I like you. It scares me more than a little to say it, but it's the truth. So, I'm going to take the risk and put it out there. But I don't know what to do about it. I have to get through Victorian Christmas. But I don't know anything about where I'm going with my life after that. If it succeeds, I go one way. If it fails, I go another. I can't drag you into that mess with me."

He listened carefully to what she said, and he knew she'd spoken honestly. She didn't know what the next year would hold for her. And if she couldn't save her business, that meant she'd lose her job and her ability to pay her rent and all the other bills that went along with being an adult. It had to scare her. He could respect that.

He'd been in love with her from afar for so long. But he hadn't pushed any of that for more than a year.

He wasn't going to push now—but he wasn't going to just raise a white flag and be content to have shared nothing more than one kiss.

"Here's what we do. We drop the tailgate on my truck, and we eat lunch. This is a season of hope. It's a season that reminds us that nothing is impossible—not even a baby in a manger coming to save the world. Nothing's impossible—not saving your store, not anything. We'll have lunch, and then we'll fight for what we want…together."

5

———

Channel Four's satellite truck had set up across the street from Provident Square, and a small crowd of familiar faces started to gather near the city's official Christmas tree.

Jessica smoothed the front of her winter white pants. She'd worn her favorite cowl neck red sweater today and affixed a crystal-covered holly-shaped brooch to the edge of the collar where it draped over her shoulder. It was one of her favorite outfits and looked festive.

Something in her stomach grumbled. She couldn't exactly place why, though. She'd just snacked on Café Provident's trial run of wassail and roasted chestnuts, so she didn't think hunger was the right answer. She'd stayed up late into the night practicing her notes and mentally reviewing all her tips for being interviewed that Bradley had taught her at their lunch on the beach. She could actually say she felt confident about how she'd do when the camera turned on.

But that memory brought to mind the source of her one chief concern.

Bradley.

And that kiss.

The thought of going on live TV with a Houston-based TV station didn't make her nervous. But reliving that kiss in her mind for the twenty-seven-thousand, nine-hundred-and-fifty-second time did.

It wasn't because she regretted the kiss, either. No, after all those mental replays, she realized her thoughts and fears circled around the fact that she *didn't* regret it. Not one bit. That fact surprised her.

Maybe Samantha had been right. She usually was.

Jessica hadn't dated anyone in years. In fact, she hadn't thought of dating anyone in years. She'd grown up working in the store, then gone to college and poured her time into her studies and her work at the store—there hadn't been much left over for anyone or anything else. After college, she did have a few casual connections, but nothing that lasted more than a few dates at the most. No one seemed to understand her obligation to her family's legacy and the hours that owning a retail store required. If you didn't put in crazy hours, every day of the week, you would not be successful—especially in a tourist town. There were no days off.

Four years ago, everything came to an abrupt halt when her mother was diagnosed with cancer. Any hours that weren't spent at the store were spent with her mother, both taking care of her and soaking up the time that remained for Jessica to sit in her presence.

And then, in that cold, bitter Christmas season two years ago, Linda Bretton lost her battle with cancer.

Nothing had been the same since.

Jessica could barely hold together her own heart, much less take the responsibility of investing in someone else's.

And then along came Bradley Thorpe. He'd just come in Bretton's on the Boardwalk to tear down a poster. She had no idea that at that moment, he'd start tearing down walls she'd had built around her heart for years.

"All ready for your big debut, my dear?" Anita Sullivan usually walked with a dignified, even footfall. But if Jessica didn't know better, she'd say it sounded like her mentor had scampered up behind her, full of excitement.

Jessica stepped off the last step of the Bretton's building and down to the historic slate sidewalk.

"I think so." She took in a deep breath.

"Think so?" Anita nailed Jessica with an askance glance. "You've got about 90 seconds of walking between here and where the news crew is set up in front of that Christmas tree. You'd better be ready."

"I'm ready for the interview, Anita. I've been practicing."

Anita adjusted a tote bag with a quote from Charles Dickens on her shoulder. "So, what's bothering you?"

"What if—after all the planning and everything else—what if it doesn't work? What if it all fails?"

"You could. That's true. That's a risk you take when you go after something your heart wants—but you don't have ultimate control over the outcome." The older woman reached out and placed a hand on Jessica's forearm. "But my dear, you could also soar like one of our island's beloved pelicans. You could spread your wings and glide on your way to the horizon. You could go farther than you've ever dreamed. This is a season of hope. And it all started with a dream."

Jessica wrinkled her nose slightly. "What do you mean?"

"Christmas. It started with a dream. An angel appeared to Mary in a dream and told her she'd been chosen to bring the son of God into the world. She never would have aspired to something like that on her own, never would have thought it was possible. But she knew the truth in her heart. She knew she could do what was asked of her—even if it seemed crazy or hard. And you know the truth in your heart, too. It's been hard for all of us here in Port Provident since Hurricane Hope. So much rebuilding. So many stops and starts. You've had your own trials —and I know you're at the end of your garland with all the worry on your shoulders this season. But wouldn't it be lovely if Hurricane Hope was more than just a name on a storm? Wouldn't it be lovely if the dream in your heart brings us all some hope this season? Your friends and neighbors need hope right now. They need you."

She hadn't quite thought about it like that. "You know, Anita, I haven't been to church in years. I own a retail store in a tourist town. I have to be open for tourists on Sundays."

Anita gave Jessica's forearm another knowing pat. "The miracle of Christmas is for those who believe in their hearts. Not just for those who sit in pews. The miracle of Christmas is love. And love is for everyone who opens their hearts to the truth of love, my sweet girl."

"I don't even know my own heart anymore, Anita."

"That's okay, my dear. I know someone who does."

Jessica turned her head and looked toward the scene in Provident Square. The city's Christmas tree was lit brightly. Everything was moving into place to be a festive backdrop for the on-camera interview.

A camel walked just behind the central tree, guided to a live nativity scene by a member of First Central Church of Port Provident. She looked at the camel's escort a little more closely as he brought the tall, golden animal near the manger where the baby representing Jesus would soon lay.

It wasn't just any member of First Provident. It was Bradley Thorpe.

Anita followed Jessica's gaze across the street.

"You know, Jessica," she said with a smile as sweet as a gumdrop on a sugar cookie, "that gentleman with the camel knows who I'm talking about. And something tells me he might know a little about your heart, too."

Jessica didn't have long to reflect on the truth of Anita's words. She was about to be upstaged by a camel in the town square. It figured.

"Bradley, can you control your camel?" Jessica hissed in a loud whisper as the golden-haired mischief maker tried to nibble at the hem of her sweater.

"Doubtful. Have you ever tried to reason with a Bactrian?" Bradley whispered back to Jessica from his spot behind a hump.

Jessica swatted at the probing camel snout. "That's your problem. The camel doesn't trust you. You're dissing him."

"How on earth would you know that?"

"He's not a Bactrian. A Bactrian camel has two humps. Your friend there is a dromedary."

Bradley inspected the camel's physique, then suddenly leaned low under the camel and then popped back up. "He's also actually a she. So I'm not the only one the camel doesn't trust."

Right now, Jessica could confidently say she didn't want to kiss Bradley. More to the point, she sort of wanted to slap him.

"Whatever," she said. "Can you just stop your friend from trying to eat my sweater? This is live TV. I can't forget what I need to say because I'm distracted by some animal who came straight out of a midnight clear."

"I'll do my best," Bradley said, moving back into place behind the camel hump as David Carbajal walked toward Jessica.

Jessica had no idea how the lead anchor for Channel Four turned out for her story. It seemed to go against all the news station hierarchy.

But she needed to just go with it. People would tune in to see what David Carbajal thought of things—they always did. He was the most respected broadcaster in the area.

"Are you ready?" he asked Jessica as he took a microphone from a member of his team and handed it to her."

Jessica took a deep breath. She wanted to believe she was ready. That would have to be enough for now. "I think so. Thank you for coming today. I didn't know you did spots out in the field anymore."

David fiddled with an earpiece. "I usually don't, but I overheard some of our producers talking about this and decided to take it for myself. My daughter, Celina, lives here in Port Provident. Covering this gives me the chance to surprise her at school for lunch."

For some reason, that made Jessica relax. He wasn't here because of anything crazy. He just wanted to see his daughter. He had a completely logical explanation for covering this particular story.

They both got into place. Jessica made sure to stand a few steps away from Bradley's curious camel. The backdrop of nativity-themed animals and small children dressed as shepherds made a very touching backdrop.

Jessica wished that they'd been able to pull together something that looked more Victorian, but costumes were still being ordered and backdrops were being hastily built in the wee hours by locals after their day jobs concluded. It was all hands on deck to bring the Victorian Christmas to life, but they would need every second until the opening to pull it off.

So, for now, Bradley had arranged for First Provident to set up their live nativity scene, and Jessica was grateful for the church's help. And for Bradley's help. What would she have done without him? He arranged the interview, then he set up a scene to make it look beautiful and festive and inviting for viewers.

Every time she thought about how much Bradley had done for her, her heart began to soar. Then sober reality pulled it back down. She didn't have the luxury of following her heart into the clouds right now. She had a very real job to do. This was beyond just saving Bretton's now—she might have even talked herself out of the Victorian Christmas if it was just about her.

People and businesses all across Port Provident were counting on the Victorian Christmas to provide a spark to their holiday season.

They were counting on Jessica.

They needed Jessica.

She didn't really know how to do any of this. But she did know she couldn't let them down.

As she told Bradley, she'd been faking being holly and jolly for quite a while now. She could do it for five more minutes while the camera rolled.

The cameraman waved his hand, then counted down with his fingers and pointed directly at David. When a large red light turned on at the top of the camera, David began to speak.

"Well, I'm usually in the studio, but today I'm in the holiday spirit and I'm down here in Port Provident talking about the upcoming Victorian Christmas Carol weekend with Jessica Bretton of Bretton's on the Boardwalk, a Port Provident institution." David pivoted slightly toward Jessica and the camel gave a sniff in the TV personality's direction. "Thanks for joining me today."

"It's a pleasure to be out here talking about getting Port Provident into the Christmas spirit."

Jessica hadn't realized it, but a crowd had gathered around the square. She saw many familiar faces—not just downtown business owners, but people from all over Port Provident.

Suddenly, she felt energized. These friends and neighbors were here to show their support for Victorian Christmas. They were counting on her to spread the word.

"So, tell me about the idea for Victorian Christmas. The annual Santas on the Street event was canceled, so how did this come about?"

Jessica tried to smile. People on TV liked to see smiles.

Out of the corner of her eye, though, she saw Mayor Angela Ruiz moving through the small gathered crowd. Suddenly, Jessica felt the flutter in her chest of a rapidly-increasing heartrate.

Why was Angela here?

She'd already made it clear she wasn't a fan of Jessica's idea.

Would she step in the interview and say something?

Jessica knew it was far-fetched to even think that the mayor would run into the shot and grab the microphone. But stranger things had happened.

Like having a store which had been around for a century now being on the verge of closing its doors.

With that reminder, Jessica took a steadying breath and began to relay the history of the Port Provident Ladies' Musicale Society and the original event of 1890. She took David Carbajal and his audience through the growth of the event and described how it came to an end after the Great Storm of 1910.

"We've been through our own great storm this year, but instead of bringing things to an end, to me, it feels like the right time to pick up a tradition like this again. It is being fully coordinated at the local business level. Each business here in the downtown district is putting their own spin on a Victorian Christmas. You'll get to try out wassail and roasted chestnuts at Café Provident. Provident Youth Theatre will be staging *A Christmas Carol* several times during the weekend. And of course, Bretton's on the Boardwalk will be your home for holiday cheer."

Jessica hoped her description had been enough to convince people to come. *Please, God, let it be enough.*

The prayer—brief as it was—shocked Jessica a bit. She wasn't the praying type. She wasn't the church type. As she'd told Anita, she didn't have anything against churches, but running a retail business didn't make it easy to get there on Sundays.

Maybe Anita's words about Mary and Christmas had rubbed off. That's the best explanation Jessica could give herself right now.

"Is there anything else that our viewers can expect down here? I know the mayor has been speaking lately about how Port Provident is open for business. But is the recovery truly in full swing? Or will this just be a handful of stores within a few blocks taking part?"

A chill shot through Jessica's veins as her heart plummeted. She'd expected the anchor to close with a softball question and then wrap it up and tell people to come out.

Instead, now, the whole event kind of sounded lame.

It sounded like a block party.

No one was going to get in their car and drive from Houston for wassail at a block party.

Jessica should have known better. So much for that prayer. It wasn't enough. Nothing would be enough.

She shouldn't have pinned all her hopes on this crazy idea. It had sounded good to her because she was desperate for something—anything—to sound like it could save the family business. And so she'd built the chance at pulling off the Victorian Christmas to be something it wasn't—in her heart, she'd made it out to be something it could never be.

She should have listened to her head instead of Anita and Bradley and their churchy talk…and above all, she shouldn't have listened to her stupid, naïve heart.

Some things *weren't* worth the risk.

"Jessica?" David Carbajal tipped his microphone in her direction, as though he assumed she wasn't speaking because her microphone was broken.

It wasn't the microphone that had broken. It was her dream that she could make this work.

"Yes—this is something the whole island is excited about." Becca

Collins, director of the Port Provident Animal Shelter, stepped out of the crowd and walked over to Jessica and took the microphone. "The Port Provident Animal Shelter will be there with several pets who need a fur-ever home for the holidays. And Dr. Ross Reeder will be on site giving information about a program he has to match homes with combat dogs who are retiring from the Army. It will be a great chance for people to come out and learn about how to foster or adopt the perfect animal for their family."

All Jessica could do was smile and take a deep breath of relief.

David nodded and turned toward Becca. "How's the shelter doing after the storm?"

"Thanks to the Peoples Property Group, we are doing great. We're moving into a new location, thanks to their generosity and some assistance from our friends at Helping Hands Homes."

Becca pointed directly at Matt McGregor, the executive director of the organization.

"And who's that?" David asked.

Matt came forward as Becca introduced him. "Matt is a Port Provident native who now lives in Austin, but he's come back with Helping Hands Homes to make a huge impact in our community by rebuilding one hundred damaged homes by Christmas."

David put out his hand and Matt shook it as he came to stand close to Becca. "So, tell the viewers at home—what number are you on?"

"With just a few weeks to go, we have ninety-four restorations complete. I actually expect to exceed our goal by one or two."

David looked back at the camera, then turned again toward Matt. "And will you be part of the Victorian Christmas, as well?"

"Well, I'll probably be working," Matt chuckled. "But I was just talking with Princess Anneliese de Cotriaro of San Petro—her capital city is a sister city to Port Provident and she came here for a while to help us rebuild and raise funds—and she said that she plans to come back for the holidays to see this."

Jessica felt her jaw drop slightly. She knew Princess Anneliese had raised an incredible amount of money for Port Provident, but now that she'd gone home, Jessica had never dreamed that the royal would keep tabs on little things going on in the city like this.

"In fact—Jessica, will there be a parade? Because I definitely think the princess would love to be a part."

Before Jessica could make up an answer to Matt's question, Samantha slipped out of the crowd and stepped forward within view of the camera. "A parade is part of the event's history. Starting in 1901, members of the British royal family were appearing as the grand marshals of the Victorian Christmas parade to celebrate the connection to Queen Victoria and honor her life, as she had just passed away earlier that year. Not only are we investigating how to put together a parade, but I've been talking with Home and Hearth TV about coming back to film the weekend. They were here last year, before the storm, and they've expressed an interest in following up with our city. I can't think of a better event to highlight our recovery from Hurricane Hope than this."

"I agree," David said. "It sounds like this could be one of the biggest weekends Port Provident has seen in years."

Jessica noted an air of enthusiasm in his voice that hadn't been there only moments ago. Once the others stepped forward out of the audience, it gave a whole new level of credibility to the event. David Carbajal had noticed. Maybe his viewers would too.

Maybe Christmas could be saved after all.

Maybe Jessica's Christmas wish could come true.

Maybe hasty prayers could move mountains—or sand dunes, as the case may be.

"Well, that's it from here in Port Provident. Be sure you come down next weekend for Victorian Christmas. All of Port Provident is turning out to make it a success. All they need is you to come down, spread some Christmas cheer, and support the city's recovery from Hurricane Hope."

David wrapped it all up in a way that made Jessica want to hug him. Yes. That was exactly it. He said it perfectly.

As Jessica turned to shake his hand to conclude the interview, something held her back.

This time, it wasn't her feelings or her fear.

It was a camel. Specifically, a dromedary with a small bit of attitude.

Jessica twisted around as much as she could with her sweater pinned between camel's teeth. Bradley shrugged.

"Don't worry. I'm not quitting the day job." He flashed her a smile that would have melted the most stubborn winter snow as he coaxed the camel into letting go. Looking at the joy and relief on his face turned her feet into pools of hot chocolate. "And, so, it seems, neither are you. Nice job, Bretton. The people will turn out for this. Wait and see."

Wait and see.

Only a few more days until they'd know if Bradley's prediction would come true.

She could wait a few more days. She had so much work to do in the meantime.

And she couldn't help but wish to see that smile on his face again —and soon.

Bradley hadn't seen Jessica in three days, but as he helped First Provident set up for tonight's official Christmas pageant on the square, he realized his eyes were glued to the Bretton's front door across the way.

He felt a bit like a stalker elf, but he needed to see Jessica. He'd spent the last twenty-four hours telling himself that she was just busy. She wasn't avoiding him.

Or so he hoped. If Santa was going to be here tonight, he'd sit in the jolly old man's lap and ask him for just one Christmas wish— another kiss with Jessica Bretton.

He didn't want much.

Just a chance. Just a kiss. And maybe, just a little bit of forever.

"I see you hiding back there. I was hoping you'd bring your pet camel with you."

Bradley stepped from behind the Christmas tree and was relieved to hear that Jessica's voice sounded completely relaxed—no signs of second-guessing, regrets, or stress. She must have been able to think about something other than the kiss on the beach.

"She's coming on the next trailer. I think there's a few sheep and donkeys coming with her too. She's been a little cantankerous today—did you know that camels spit?—and that probably won't go well with that pretty holly brooch you're wearing."

She touched the red and green crystals lightly with her fingers. "It belonged to my mother. My father had it custom-made by one of our long-time vendors."

"Then we definitely wouldn't want to get camel spit on it." Bradley gave a mock-scathing look over his shoulder to the dromedary. "Hey, the live nativity will be up and running in about an hour. I've done my part for the setup. Now it's just a matter of waiting for the animals to get here. Would you like to walk through it with me tonight? Maybe we can go across the street to Soda Pop's and get a shake or something while we wait."

Bradley held his breath just slightly. It was the first time he'd asked her to do anything by themselves since that kiss on the beach. He reminded himself of the promise he'd made to himself. No more silence. Jessica needed someone who would stand by her.

He could do that.

He *would* do that.

Well, as long as she said yes to a chocolate peppermint shake and an evening with sheep, camels, and baby Jesus.

When they arrived at their destination, Bradley was pleased to see that a short line snaked around the inside of Soda Pop.

"It's exciting to see people lined up in here for a change," Jessica said in a lowered voice as they waited. "Every time I've been in here since the hurricane, there have been two or three other people, tops. It gives me some encouragement that things are going to work out."

Bradley indulged himself in his new favorite pastime, settling his arm around Jessica's shoulders. "They are. You've got a good plan. I know you and your fellow business owners can execute it. You've just got to have faith."

She gave a sharp, stilted nod of her head. "Can I ask you something?"

"Sure. Anything."

"Before the TV interview, Anita said something similar to what you're saying."

Jessica turned and faced him in the line. Her eyes were wide and Bradley the oversized pupils made them look very dark—almost like the camel's, right down to the long, graceful fringe of lashes.

He nodded, prompting her to push through the pause and continue.

"I just don't have that in me anymore. I explained to Anita that I haven't been to church in years. When you're the person who has the keys to the store, and you've got to be open on the days the most tourists are present, well… it just gets hard. I quit even trying after my mom died. Didn't seem like there was much of a point, anyway."

They reached the front of the line and Bradley ordered a peppermint chocolate shake for both of them. While it always struck him as counter-intuitive to buy an ice cream-based treat during the winter, he couldn't deny that since he'd come to Port Provident, these once-a-year specialties had come to symbolize one of his favorite things about the holidays.

"Come on over here with me." Bradley kept his arm tucked around Jessica's shoulders as they strolled back across the street to Provident Square. The dark sky of evening had settled above them, and the light from the stars above provided a nice counterpoint to the twinkle of the small white lights wrapped around the Christmas tree in the corner of the square.

Jessica sipped on her shake through the oversized straw as they walked, not saying much. They walked down a path designed to look like a street in Bethlehem. Then they came to the replica stable.

Bradley squeezed the top of her shoulder gently. "Stop right here. Do you see it?"

She turned her head from side to side. "No, I guess I don't. What's 'it'?"

"Her." He pointed at a young woman dressed in a plain blue dress with a white robe. "She's just like you."

"Mary? I don't understand. I don't have a baby."

"No. But I'm not talking about that. By all accounts, she was a nice young woman. She was engaged. He was gainfully employed as a carpenter. She knew what her life was going to look like, what was expected of her. You've always known that about yourself, too. Bretton's has been in your family for generations. Have you ever wanted to do anything else?"

She hesitated before replying. "Well, no. Not really. I'm an only child, and so was my dad. If I didn't take over Bretton's, who would? It's just in my blood, I guess."

"So you do understand." He continued. "One day, she was told her life was going to be very different than those thoughts and dreams she'd held since she was born. Her family wouldn't be there. She'd have to do it on her own. She'd wind up needing to be resourceful— like using a feeding trough filled with hay—and she'd need to believe in her own abilities. But she wouldn't be alone, either."

"Well, sure. God, right?"

"Absolutely, but more than that, God gave the same dream to one special person in her life. One person who would be alongside her and who would understand." He turned and looked right in Jessica's wide, dark blue eyes. "The holidays are about hope, Jessica—and perhaps this holiday even more than any Port Provident has seen before. You may be far from your family and life may not look like you've always thought it would, but you do have someone who understands. Me."

She wiggled a little, and Bradley took the hint to pull his arm back down to his side.

"I want to say yes, Bradley. But I feel like I'm imposing on you or something."

His heart sank a little. Maybe neither of them would get their Christmas wishes this year.

Or maybe he needed to take his own advice and just believe.

"Jessica, close your eyes." His voice dropped to a whisper. People swirled in the square all around them, but his words were only for her. "Believe."

He pulled little more closely toward her. Their breath mingled in puffs above the chill of the peppermint shakes.

"In what?" She sounded a little confused, but she didn't open her eyes. "In God, in Christmas, in miracles?"

Bradley lowered his head and kissed her softly. He tasted the quick bite of the peppermint between them.

He held his breath, waiting. Had he made the right decision?

Jessica leaned toward him and deepened the kiss. She didn't pull away. And then he knew.

When the kiss was over, he brushed his thumb across her lower lip, then tucked a strand of blonde hair behind her ear.

"In us," he whispered.

Jessica's eyes reflected the light of the Bethlehem star over the live nativity. She smiled back at him, and he watched an age-old knowledge settle into her gaze.

"I do," she said simply, and it was enough for Bradley.

The chance to show her how much he cared was the best Christmas gift he'd never dared to ask for.

6

———————

The rest of the week passed in a blur. Bradley had stayed at Jessica's side all week. He ran errands, he brought her lunch during the day, and made sure she got dinner at night. He even called after she'd gone home to make sure she went to bed on time.

And on Friday night, when she thought her eyes would stay permanently crossed from looking at spreadsheets full of details for both the event and Bretton's bottom line, Bradley rescued her and drove her out to see the few Christmas lights that had started to pop up across town.

Afterwards, Bradley took her to the Point Provident lighthouse, where they sat under blankets and looked at the stars.

And then he kissed her until she completely forgot about spreadsheets and bank accounts and wassail and chestnuts.

Jessica didn't remember a time when Bradley hadn't been by her side. And she didn't want to think about how it might be after the Victorian Christmas. She knew he'd be more involved with his restructured job over at the Park Board—it only made sense—but she hoped they could still find a way for dinners together and stargazing at the edge of Port Provident.

Oh, and the kisses. She needed to make sure they'd always have time for those.

But until then, they'd have wassail and choirs. And pet adoptions and a princess waving to the crowd. They weren't able to pull off a full parade—Bradley couldn't find a loophole to make that one work—but Princess Anneliese had said she'd make herself available for photos at the square in the afternoon.

The generosity of the community had overwhelmed her. Port Provident had risen above the storm and come together with a deep sense of Christmas spirit that would not soon be forgotten.

And it never would have happened without Anita's photos and Bradley's planning.

She owed them both a deep debt of gratitude for her renewed faith in what was to come.

But first, she needed to make it through today.

Jessica looked over the stack of flyers on the corner of the front counter at Bretton's one last time. Each participating merchant was listed, along with the themes at each location. She would be hosting photos with Queen Victoria and a Victorian-style Santa Claus.

Everything was in order for A Victorian Christmas. All the brainstorming, collaborating, and days of frantic promoting had led to this one afternoon. All that Jessica had left to do was to open the doors.

She walked around brightly-decorated Christmas trees and bins of ornaments.

Stopping just short of the door, a display of ceramic nativity sets from Italy caught her eye. They were a staple at Bretton's—one of the store's best-selling items. But as she slowed, Jessica realized she saw them in a whole new light.

Jessica picked up the figurine of Mary and held it in her right hand, then picked up the figurine representing Joseph and held it in her left. She sighed. Of course, she'd known the Christmas story since childhood, but she'd never really *known* Mary and Joseph—or thought much about them. They'd been names on a page in her grandmother's Bible.

But as she held the glazed ceramic figurines in her hands, Jessica saw them as if for the first time. A young mother wanting the best for her small family, a new entrepreneur trying to get his carpentry business off the ground so he could support his loved ones. They'd been real people once.

With the figurines still tucked tightly in her hands, Jessica closed her eyes and let the voice in her mind whisper her most guarded thoughts and fears…and hopes.

Dear God, the people I care about the most seem to be reminding me that you're still in the business of miracles. I hope so. I need one today. The bills are as high as I am tall, and the money is as low as a tree skirt draped across the floor. I want to hope. I want to believe. I want the miracle to be made real and undeniable.

Her heart pounded with adrenaline as she wrapped up the prayer. Slowly, she placed the figurines back in their rightful spot in the stable.

Jessica took a step back and looked at the little family and their animals. Then, with a light touch, she reached back inside the stable and turned Mary and Joseph slightly so that they were facing one another.

They were there for each other—just as she realized Bradley was there for her.

Her thoughts turned back to him.

Bradley had been there all along. He'd brought her cups of coffee and brought her information on opportunities from the Park Board for more than a year. He always listened to her ideas and followed up to let her know if an action had been taken on her suggestions.

When she'd tried to give up on this crazy idea—he wouldn't let her.

When she'd come clean about her family, her financial situations, and her fears, he'd held her.

And then he'd kissed her.

There had been a miracle in front of her all along. Samantha and Whitt and Anita had known, but she hadn't seen it. What else had she missed?

Jessica unlocked the door to the store and propped it wide open with a doorstop. The sounds of a choir on the street singing *O Little Town of Bethlehem* caught her ears.

The hopes and fears of all the years are met in thee tonight…

That summed up all the thoughts in her mind perfectly. Hope and fear.

But as she saw people walking down the street and ducking into shops, Jessica made a decision.

She would choose hope.

It seemed like every business owner of every kind in Port Provident had stopped Bradley today. But eventually, he made his way to the sidewalk just in front of the steps of Bretton's.

"Bradley—wait up. I need to talk to you!" He recognized the high-pitched voice of Deborah Moore, his new boss. He'd been officially transferred to her management, effective yesterday.

He stopped in the middle of the sidewalk and tried to compose his face before she caught up to him.

"What is all this? The City Council voted down any holiday events. I went up to the office to see what I could find out about it, and Brent was there. He said you'd been active in planning this. Care to explain what is going on?"

He leaned against the Bretton's stair rail. "Looks like a bunch of downtown business owners are having events today."

"They can't have events today." Deborah placed her hands on her hips, looking entirely out of place among the relaxed tourists milling all about.

"Why not? The city is generally not in the business of telling people they can't have sales or special promotions. And after all, it is the Christmas season. You'd generally expect lots of sales, would you not?"

"This is not a sale."

"You're right, it's not." A familiar voice came from just inside the doorway. "This is a collective celebration of hope and joy for the citizens of Port Provident and beyond. We've had a rough fall and winter. The downtown merchants association decided to come up with something fun to lift everyone's spirits."

"And you are?" Deborah looked over the top of her red-framed glasses.

Jessica walked down the steps and put out her hand in introduction. "Jessica Bretton, owner of Bretton's on the Boardwalk. I don't believe we've met."

"Deborah Moore, director of the Port Provident Convention and Visitors Bureau." Her eyes sized Jessica up. "I'm Bradley's boss."

Jessica smiled sweetly, but her voice carried plenty of confidence and sass. Bradley loved hearing her come into her own—especially in front of the manager he didn't want or need. "That's funny, he really hasn't mentioned you. But I hope you enjoy your afternoon down here. You can have your photo taken with Queen Victoria in my store. And there will be a performance of *A Christmas Carol* by PYT—the Provident Youth Theatre company in the square closer to sunset."

Deborah did not match Jessica's overt saccharine in her reply. "There absolutely will not be anything of the kind."

"Why not?" Bradley jumped back in the conversation.

"There's no permit on file for any such thing."

She looked at Bradley with a very level gaze. It made a low-grade fire flash in his belly.

"And if you do issue such a thing, Bradley, you may submit your resignation along with it. I'm going to get the police to get these crowds off the streets. The City Council said they didn't want anything like this, and you facilitated it instead. Be in my office first thing Monday morning."

Deborah turned and walked away before Bradley could respond. He couldn't get his jaw unclenched enough to say anything.

"She's going to shut it down?" Jessica grabbed Bradley's arm. Instantly, his anger melted and his focus shifted right back to where it should have been—on Jessica and the Victorian Christmas event.

"She'll probably try. That's just how she operates."

"Bradley, she can't. Things are going well. Today's the best day

I've had since Labor Day weekend, and the others are telling me the same thing in emails and texts. I'm halfway to my goal. I have a chance to save my family's business. But if she shuts this down, that chance is gone—and you and I both know it's not coming back."

He pulled her close, feeling the fear she held. It was causing her entire body to tense. Instead of fitting closely beside him, she felt as straight and static as a board.

Bradley had come to this end of the downtown district to both see Jessica and to hear how her sales were going. She'd just checked both boxes. He'd pushed her into this idea. He'd prodded her to believe in herself, to believe that miracles could still happen and that hope was worth holding on to.

If she lost those feelings, he didn't know if she could ever find them again. He couldn't be responsible for that. Jessica had been through enough. She deserved more.

She deserved hope.

He didn't know what he was going to do, but he was going to see that hope returned to stay for Jessica and for Port Provident's small business owners.

"I need to grab some things at my office before she goes in there and messes everything up. Can you meet me in Provident Square in an hour?"

"As long as Donna can handle the crowd in the store for a few minutes. Although, I guess if Deborah has her way, there won't be much of a crowd in the store."

"Do me a favor, will you?" Bradley turned her shell-shocked body in his arms and held her tightly. He leaned down and planted a firm kiss square on her lips. It didn't last long, but he wanted to make sure she knew he meant what he was about to say. "Don't lose hope."

~

The sky was beginning to darken as the sun sank low. Despite Bradley's kiss and admonitions to stay positive, the new presence of approximately ten uniformed officers was having an effect on both the crowds and Jessica's spirit.

In fact, she stood on the Bretton's steps, trying to take in some breaths of cool December air to keep her from wanting to cry. Not only did it look like she would fall short of her goal number, but her problems—and the crazy fix to them—had put Bradley's job in danger. Clearly, his boss was not going to be on his side Monday.

If he lost his job, Jessica just knew she couldn't bear that guilt. She was about to lose her own job. She couldn't be responsible for getting Bradley pushed out the door too.

And of course, that would be the end of any chance at developing a relationship with Bradley. No man would want to be with the woman who got him fired from his job.

As she tried to push down the tears and the overwhelming feelings of defeat, only one refrain rang in her mind—this was absolutely *not* the most wonderful time of the year. Between this year's train wreck and her mother's holiday season death two years before, Jessica realized maybe *she* wasn't the fake.

Maybe Christmas itself was the fake.

Suddenly, the faint jingle of sleigh bells dusted the air like salt from a shaker. Jessica had to be hearing things. There were no sleigh bells on the agenda for today's events—and quite honestly, there was no longer an agenda of events, thanks to Deborah Moore.

Jessica looked down the block and saw Deborah standing under a flickering gas-lit lamppost, talking to a police officer. Mayor Angela Ruiz stood a half-step back, her arms crossed. She kept looking across the street at the gathered crowd as her daughter tugged at her sleeve and pointed at the animals.

The mayor gave her daughter a dismissive wave of her hand and continued to follow Deborah's spirited conversation.

Jessica's spirits sank even lower, even though the sound of the mystery jingle bells stayed constant.

"*Ho ho ho*! Merry Christmas! *Ho Ho Ho*! Listen up, boys and girls, Santa has an announcement!"

The voice echoed loud and clear down the street, bouncing off the multi-story historic stone and stucco buildings on both sides. Jessica couldn't stop herself from leaning forward for a look.

And then, about three blocks down, she saw it. Pargo, a chestnut brown horse that usually gave carriage rides for tourists, had a blinking set of antlers secured atop his head. Behind him, rode a white carriage wrapped in lights.

As the makeshift reindeer and sleigh got closer, Jessica was able to make out the passenger in the carriage. A man dressed as Santa was speaking into a bullhorn, repeating his announcement over and over.

It wasn't just any Santa Claus, though—it was Bradley Claus.

A flash of energy sparked in Jessica's body and pushed her down the stairs. Once her feet hit the sidewalk, she began to jog. She accelerated to a full-fledged sprint when she saw the carriage stop at the corner where Deborah stood.

She couldn't hear what was being said, but she saw Deborah point directly at Bradley and his ridiculously fake-looking beard. Two police officers stepped closer to him, one on either side of the carriage. Deborah continued to gesture wildly with her hands.

"No! Wait!" Jessica yelled out. She didn't know what she could possibly say next, but she couldn't allow Bradley to get arrested. Not for her. Not for anything. He'd been nothing but good and kind—and loving—to her.

She couldn't let this happen.

Her heart pounded from the exertion of her sprint and the adrenaline being called to the forefront by her fear over what was going to happen to Bradley.

As she reached the horse's nose, she finally could hear what they were saying.

"I don't need a permit for this, Deborah."

The woman's face was splashed with red, and she leaned forward. "It's a good thing you're working for me now because obviously, you don't know the rules. An outdoor gathering in the park must have a permit, and it must be filed two weeks in advance unless it meets the criteria for an emergency situation. And you playing Santa Claus is absolutely not an emergency situation."

Bradley pulled a piece of paper out of his pocket. Jessica could see the yellow and pink duplicate and triplicate copies waving in the breeze under the main white copy.

"The First Central Church of Port Provident has a permit for their live nativity performance in Provident Square every night this week. And tonight, they've invited some special guests to join them. The PYT will be performing scenes from A Christmas Carol. You can't stop these people from coming to watch their performance. There's no need for a police force out here. These are people coming to peacefully watch a nativity scene and Tiny Tim. If they happen to visit some of our wonderful local shops while they're here, then that's great too. You're the director of the Convention and Visitors Bureau. I don't think City Council is going to appreciate you bringing some kind of martial law down on our tourists and citizens."

He waved the permit paperwork in her face for added emphasis.

Without a word, Deborah waved a dismissive hand at the officers, then turned on her heel. "Monday," she said with gritted teeth. "Monday."

Angela Ruiz plucked the paper from Bradley's hand. "This is a real permit?"

"Laura Riley issued it two weeks ago. It's as legit as it comes."

She held it up. "Who's cleaning all this up afterwards?"

Bradley folded the paper and stuffed it back in the pocket of his red coat.

"The Peoples Family Foundation is covering it. Diana Peoples has gotten the groundskeeping crew from the Peoples Property Group to work some overtime," Bradley explained succinctly.

Angela's daughter tugged on her hand. "Mom, we're going to miss the candy cane demonstration at Island Confectionary."

"It looks like you've covered your bases," the mayor said. "I don't know what else Deborah has, though."

"Me neither. But I do know what Port Provident has now."

"What's that?" The mayor had already taken two steps toward the candy shop.

"Hope. This is a holiday of hope." With a smile hiding in his fake white curls, he extended a hand to Jessica.

"Your sleigh, my dear."

Jessica placed her palm in his gloved one and boosted herself up into the lighted carriage.

"To the square, Donner," Bradley said.

"That's not Donner," Jessica said with a laugh. "That's Pargo."

He placed a finger deliberately over her lips. "*Sssh.* Don't tell him."

After a very short trot, they reached the square, which had become full of visitors in a short time. Deborah's scare tactics and the police she'd brought with her hadn't scared them completely off—Bradley's Santa notification had worked.

He hopped out of the carriage, then helped Jessica out. Hand in hand, they slowly made their way through the crowd to the front.

"But what about Monday?" Jessica squeezed Bradley's hand, more looking for reassurance for herself that he didn't hate her for getting him in hot water.

"What about it?" Bradley shrugged.

"But what's going to happen to you on Monday?"

He tilted his head and looked right in her eyes. All the fear she'd felt melted away like a snowman on the beach. "I have no idea. The mayor seemed okay with everything. I don't know what else Deborah has up her sleeve. But I'm not worried. This is a season of hope, remember?"

"People keep telling me that." For the first time since she'd clutched the nativity figurines this morning, Jessica felt the stored-up tension leave her body.

"And besides," Bradley leaned his head in close to hers. She could feel the warm whisper of his breath on her cheek along with the cool breeze of the December night. "I can always come get a job at Bretton's on the Boardwalk. I have a feeling they're going to be back and better than ever as Port Provident continues to recover from Hurricane Hope."

He raised a hand and tangled it in the hair at the back of her neck, then kissed her. At first, the sensation fluttered through her body as gentle as a snowflake, but quickly, it fanned into something that reminded her of the fire at the café that was creating batch after batch of roasted chestnuts. She could feel the growing warmth throughout her body, and she leaned in closer to Bradley.

After a moment, he pulled back. He smiled as he looked straight in her eyes.

From the stage where PYT was finishing their performance, Tiny Tim raised a crutch. "God bless us, every one!"

Jessica looked at the little boy on the stage. She turned her head and looked at the other end of the square, where the animals gathered around the manger. And then she looked straight in the eyes of the man who still held her warmly in his arms.

For the first time in years, she saw the answer to her prayers right in front of her.

She looked over Bradley's shoulder, unable to take her eyes off Mary—the young woman she'd been shown to have so much in common with. This Christmas, she'd been given two of the gifts that had come to earth on that night in Bethlehem. She'd been given the miracle of hope and love.

And life would never be the same.

EPILOGUE

"**J**essica, Home and Hearth wants to interview you. Can you come over here for a minute?" Samantha yelled down the street. Her voice sounded louder than Santa's shout from the back of the sleigh.

"Coming!" Jessica hoped her reply carried above the hustle and bustle of the crowd.

The Victorian Christmas had expanded to cover two weekends this year. People had come from all across Texas to take part. Jessica had even wrapped up a delicate blown-glass angel for a family from New Orleans about an hour ago.

"Can you believe what's happened in just a year?" Bradley jogged up to her from his post as emcee on the main stage.

"No, I really can't. I just wanted to save Bretton's. But look what's come out of it." Jessica waved her hand for emphasis.

Bradley took it and placed a firm kiss just below her knuckles. "Go do your interview, but come and see me when you're finished, okay?"

Jessica nodded. "I'll try, but Donna needs a break at six o'clock."

"I'll get someone to cover it for her. That new girl should be able to handle it. What was her name?"

"Gina."

"Got it. I'll see you in a bit." Bradley started to walk in the direction of Bretton's.

Jessica stopped next to a man dressed as Jacob Marley and posed for a picture. The Home and Hearth crew came to film her interacting with the crowd. And when Reid Knight, their TV personality, began to ask questions, Jessica found herself utterly relaxed. She made jokes with her answers and invited the entire country to come next year and see what Port Provident was about.

What a difference three-hundred-and-sixty-five days made.

Last December, she needed the entire community behind her to finish an interview with local TV. Now, she breezed through filming with a national powerhouse as though she carried a Screen Actors Guild card.

As Jessica criss-crossed the street that had been closed to traffic, she realized that she was better because of this community. The mentors who shared history with her. The fellow business owners who realized that a rising tide lifted all of their ships. The others in the community who wanted to be a part of something that brought holiday joy to busy hearts. The friends who told her to face her fears. The role models who shared their faith.

And one man who'd shared his heart.

She saw Bradley on stage, getting ready to introduce the First Provident choir for some more caroling. Jessica's heart swelled. Bradley now led tourism for the entire island. He reported directly to Mayor Angela Ruiz, who had seen first-hand how he'd been able to work out the details and put together an event that met the needs of the recovering city and the businesses at the heart of the economy.

He worked for all of Port Provident now, but his whole heart belonged only to Jessica.

"Jess, come on up here," Bradley said, waving her toward the steps at the edge of the stage.

Jessica walked up and gave a half-wave to the crowd gathered around. Most of the faces were unfamiliar. But some of them, she knew by heart.

She saw Samantha and Whitt. They chatted with Ross and Rebecca

Reeder, who held the leashes of their two Labradors. Rebecca patted her growing belly and laughed at something Samantha said. At the edge of the group stood Mayor Ruiz, and her new husband, Dr. Pete Shipley—they'd finally found time to get married after the first intense phase of hurricane recovery ended. In the middle of the crowd, Diana Peoples stood between her grandson Jake's family and Anita Sullivan.

It made Jessica smile to see all the joy in front of her.

"Jessica Bretton is the one who has made this event happen. She's the fourth-generation owner of Bretton's on the Boardwalk, the only store in Port Provident where it's Christmas all year round. Jessica loves Christmas trees and ornaments. But there's one ornament you can't buy at Bretton's, and I wanted to see if Jessica could find it here on our official Port Provident Christmas tree."

Jessica looked. She saw red and gold glittery balls. Strings of twinkle lights surrounded the branches.

"Nothing looks out of the ordinary to me," she said, wondering exactly what Bradley was up to in front of all of these people.

Bradley put a hand on the small of her back and pushed her a little closer to the tree. "Look more closely. Maybe right over there."

He pointed to a branch at eye level.

Jessica realized what she'd thought was a tiny white light wasn't electrical in nature at all.

She paused, then turned to look at Bradley.

"It seems that you've found it."

He put his microphone back on the stand, then reached up and untied the red velvet ribbon that held the shining stone in place. Then he turned toward Jessica and dropped to one knee.

A quick succession of clapping came from the front row of the assembled crowd, and Jessica knew the sound came from her best friend.

"Christmas is a time when anything is possible. You can save a business. You can entertain an entire city. You can bring joy to people far and wide. And you can dream about spending forever with a woman who has done all of those things. Jessica Bretton, will you marry me?"

Jessica sucked in a deep breath of the chilled night air.

Christmas had taught her to hope, but she'd never dreamed of a gift like this. Not here, not now.

She only had one answer, but she couldn't get the words out.

Jessica nodded fiercely and put out her hand. Bradley slid the ring on her finger.

And from the back of the stage, a voice cried out, "God bless us, every one!"

Jessica knew she was more blessed than she ever thought possible. And she had a holiday filled with hope to thank for changing her life.

Did you miss a story? Read the complete Port Provident: Hurricane Hope series now!

WANT MORE OF PORT PROVIDENT?

Would you like a reader-exclusive free Port Provident story?
Join my reader society today and get A Place to Find Love, a sweet
escape Port Provident romance, available only for newsletter
subscribers!
https://www.subscribepage.com/kristenethridgenewsletter

CAN I ASK YOU FOR A SMALL FAVOR?

If you liked this story, I'd like to ask you to please leave a review. Help me spread the word about Port Provident on Amazon. Most major retailers depend on an algorithm to boost a book's visibility among readers browsing for new titles. Reviews play a major role in how those algorithms work.

I'd appreciate your help in letting other readers just like you know about *Holiday of Hope's* hope, heart, and happily-ever-after. It's not about the length of the review—even just a few words like "Good story—I enjoyed it" may seem simple, but can help other readers like you know this is a story worth picking up.

PORT PROVIDENT: HURRICANE HOPE SERIES

Read the Entire Port Provident: Hurricane Hope Series

Shelter from the Storm
The Doctor's Unexpected Family
His Texas Princess
Holiday of Hope

Love Hallmark movies? Pick up Kristen's book October Kiss, based on
the Hallmark movie viewers love! Available anywhere books are sold
—in paperback, digital, and audio!
October Kiss from Hallmark Publishing

ABOUT KRISTEN

Kristen Ethridge writes Sweet Escape Romance—stories with hope, heart and happily-ever-after—for Harlequin's Love Inspired line, Hallmark Publishing, and Laurel Lock Publishing. She's a Romance Writers of America Golden Heart Award nominee and both an Amazon Christian Fiction and Inspirational Romance #1 Best-Selling Author.

You can find Kristen in her native habitat—a Texas patio—where she's likely to be savoring the joy of a crispy taco, along with a glass of iced tea. Scents from her essential oil diffuser are also a must, since she's a certified aromatherapist. She's almost convinced her family that it's normal to talk to imaginary people, as long it goes in a book.

Find her online at http://www.kristenethridge.com and on Amazon and Bookbub. You can get a free story for signing up for her newsletter at https://www.subscribepage.com/kristenethridgenewsletter. You can also follow her adventures in writing at www.facebook.com/kristenethridgebooks.

www.kristenethridge.com
https://www.facebook.com/KristenEthridgeBooks
https://instagram.com/kristenethridge

Don't forget…if you love sweet escape romances, join Kristen's newsletter!

ACKNOWLEDGMENTS

I couldn't do this writing thing without a set of cheerleaders who continue to tell me I can do this craziness, even when I think I can't. Jessica Keller, Elana Johnson and Debra Clopton—thank you for encouraging me to do this with full focus when I really needed to know that it could work. Author friends are the best!

"Every good and perfect gift is from above, coming down from the Father of the heavenly lights, who does not change like shifting shadows…"
—JAMES 1:17 (NIV)

www.ingramcontent.com/pod-product-compliance
Lightning Source LLC
Chambersburg PA
CBHW021739190726
48288CB00009B/3112